SE JAKES

DIRTY DEEDS

EXTREME ESCAPES, LTD

I0452488

RIPTIDE PUBLISHING

Riptide Publishing
PO Box 1537
Burnsville, NC 28714
www.riptidepublishing.com

Dirty Deeds (Dirty Deeds, #1)
Copyright © 2014 by SE Jakes

Cover art: L.C. Chase, lcchase.com/design.htm
Editor: Sarah Frantz
Layout: L.C. Chase, lcchase.com/design.htm

ISBN: 978-1-62649-160-1

First edition
June, 2014

Also available in ebook:
ISBN: 978-1-62649-093-2

SE JAKES

DIRTY DEEDS

EXTREME ESCAPES, LTD

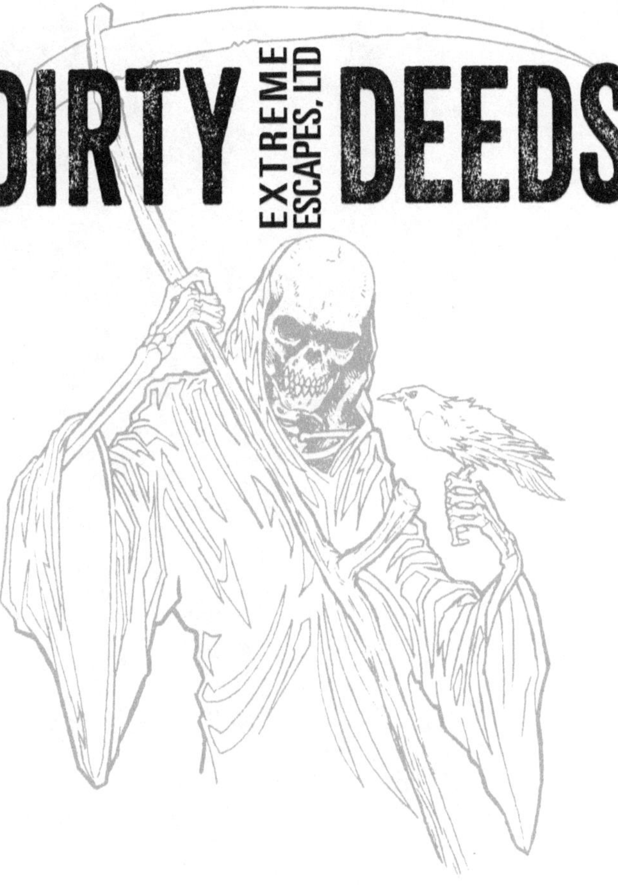

For L & C, for reasons.

Conscience is the inner voice that warns us
somebody may be looking.
-H.L. Mencken

TABLE OF CONTENTS

CHAPTER ONE

Amsterdam

Music pounded through Cillian's body like a war drum, the cacophony beating in time with his pulse as he scanned the crowded club, looking for his informant.

The dance floor was a teeming mass of bodies, undulating in sync, while the bar was more of a holding area of men cruising for their next conquest. He spotted the asshole he'd been looking for there, wound through the masses, and slid onto the empty stool next to him. Karl didn't glance at him but ordered a Jack and Coke from the bartender. When it came, Karl put four slim red straws into it and pushed it at Cillian.

Informants ran the gamut from scared to pathetic to overly dramatic. Some of them had been in it for so long, they fancied themselves some kind of honorary spy. Karl was one of those. Cillian knew the four straws were his idiotic way of saying that he'd seen the man Cillian had been tracking.

"Did you actually see him?" Cillian demanded. Karl frowned, got out his phone and showed Cillian a shadowy figure. Maybe no one else would've known who it was, but Cillian's job was to know his target better than the man knew himself. He checked the date on the photo—four days earlier—and he went with his gut. "You didn't take this."

"No," Karl admitted. "It was sent to me yesterday."

"Who sent it to you? Because they're doing a hell of a better job than you."

Karl sighed. "Shelby. He didn't say where he found it."

"Morse could be anywhere by now. This is no help to me." He pulled the straws out and tossed the drink back before he told Karl exactly how unhelpful the picture was—completely fucking worthless, in fact. "Do you have anything else?" He had to fight the urge to throw the man through the plate glass mirror behind the bar when Karl smiled, wound a hand around his shoulders, and pulled him close. More drama.

"Haven't heard from Shelby since that picture."

Cillian refrained from rolling his eyes. Barely. "You think something's wrong?"

Karl leaned into Cillian's neck like a lover would. "He was supposed to meet me two hours ago. He didn't show, and he's not answering his phone."

"Two whole hours—check the morgue," Cillian told him dryly, refusing to give away how pissed he was. Because in this game, check-ins were important for this very reason—when someone went missing, it usually wasn't an oversight. Shelby wasn't the best informant, but still, even when his intel wasn't completely on the mark, it was usually quite close, so Cillian didn't want to lose him.

He pulled away from Karl, shifted to sit with his back to the bar so he could scan the crowd.

Karl did the same, put a hand on Cillian's thigh, and said, "By the way, that dark-haired guy's still following you."

Cillian shifted his leg away from Karl's touch. "He's here?" He should've spotted Tom Boudreaux easily enough, because the man certainly wasn't a seasoned undercover operative. He was, however, a giant pain in Cillian's ass.

"No. But he was in Indonesia a couple of weeks ago, asking questions about you."

Probably because Tom was concerned that Cillian was trying to fuck his boyfriend. "And I'm just hearing this now because . . .?"

"You told me to tell you the important stuff in person." Karl gave a self-satisfied smile. "Want to dance?"

"No thanks. Knock yourself out, though."

Karl slid off the stool with a semi-disappointed look on his face. He put his hand up to his face, mimicking a phone, and mouthed, "Call me, maybe," before disappearing into the crowd.

The man *was* just like a teenaged girl. God, save him. Cillian had dealt with the man's shit because Karl was loyal. Or he had been. Cillian needed to figure out if Karl was getting lazy, or if this decidedly lacking intel was a hint at something more treacherous.

The easy thing to do would be to drop Karl from the roster, but Cillian was quite good at getting intel from his sources by any means necessary. One more performance like this, and Karl would be on the receiving end of that treatment.

Cillian ordered another drink, threw it back quickly, and then bypassed the dance floor for the safety of the back room. The hallway leading there was dark and quiet, opening into an even darker room guarded by a bouncer. The muted lighting shadowed the half-naked bodies, and the deep groans of pleasure ushered him in, overwhelming him. Bringing him back to that first heady flush of youthful power, and his first steps toward independence.

The scene laid out in front of him was a living, breathing embodiment of rough, hot sex. Not the most romantic or private setting, but Cillian had gotten used to it. He didn't necessarily like it, but fortunately, he didn't have to like something to enjoy it.

Only a few pairs and groups of three lined the walls, entwined, and Cillian briefly considered joining a couple who were watching him as they jerked each another off. But then, a strong hand clamped down on his shoulder, a grip that would normally have him turning around to break the arm holding him.

Except here, it made Cillian hard. Especially when the grip turned into a one-handed massage of Cillian's shoulder, then moved to caress the back of his neck before twisting into his hair hard enough to tilt his head to the side. He hissed when a bite landed on his neck, right before he was half-pushed, half-led to an empty corner.

And he allowed it.

He'd come in here, ready to fuck someone hard, to get rid of the anger and frustration from the meeting with Karl. And here he was, the tables turned, about to *be* fucked. In his business, surprises were never good, but hell, he was good at his job because danger turned him on. He needed it—craved it—but that didn't stop him from whipping around when the man let him go.

He didn't get much of a look beyond dark hair, broad shoulders, and height nearly equal to his own before he was shoved back against the wall and kissed, a kiss that hit him like a series of electric shocks. He closed his eyes and sank into it—it was too damned dark to get a better view than he'd gotten, and his instincts were seductively whispering to him, tempting him into believing that this was somehow safe, despite knowing that nothing ever really was. He groaned into the dark-haired man's mouth as the man rubbed his body lewdly against Cillian's, grabbing Cillian's hips and keeping their pelvises joined for a slow, hot grind.

Submissive acceptance wasn't Cillian's usual kink, but his arousal pushed him past that concern. He didn't bottom regularly, but the way this man just took charge had him intrigued. It didn't take a brain surgeon to understand why he could only let himself lose control around total strangers.

He needed this, as evidenced by the fact that neither he nor his dick was protesting.

Suddenly, the man pulled his mouth off Cillian's, and Cillian was turned roughly to face the wall. Before he could think about protesting, his pants and boxer briefs were yanked down, and two fingers trailed his ass crack.

He shuddered.

The man noticed and, in response, bit him on the side of the neck again, harder this time. Cillian would be feeling that—and no doubt his ass—for days.

A lubed finger entered him, and a second and then a third pushed in and twisted, and Cillian cried out at the combination of pleasure and pain. Tried to clutch the wall, fingers scrabbling for purchase against the smooth paint.

Giving his body over to someone he didn't know was always an exciting potential mistake, but the heightened pleasure gained from the risk was undeniable. God, it was good to feel, to know he was truly alive inside despite all the cloak-and-dagger secrecy of his job. He'd seen far too many dead men walking in his profession. After being buried in layer upon layer of undercover assignments, turning himself into whatever and whomever he needed to be to get the job done, he was relieved he could still find himself.

The other man slapped Cillian's ass—hard. As if he knew Cillian was thinking of something other than the sex.

"Fuck. Yes, I'm here," he muttered and the man bit the back of his neck lightly—a *good boy* type of thing. Before Cillian could snarl back, the man's fingers left him empty and were replaced by his cock.

Cillian cursed more as the man drove into him, the cock thick and long, filling him, impaling him as he remained helpless. He could strive to remain in control, or he could simply let go. Control was easy, but not the more fun of the two options.

The man waited a few beats once he was fully inside. Cillian took several calming breaths, then pushed back against the cock, the friction delicious as he took the man in deep.

He was rewarded by the man hissing in his ear, then yanking the collar of his shirt and biting the bare skin of his shoulder . . . and then the fucking began in earnest.

He closed his eyes and the man hit the sweet spot, immediately and often, and Cillian jolted every time. The man grabbed his hips—*I've got you*—and then Cillian couldn't move, couldn't do anything against the onslaught of thrusts. Nothing except come, which he did faster than he'd wanted to. But the climax had been building from the second the man had touched him, winding him so tightly that every single muscle screamed for release. The pleasure was so intense, so seemingly new, that Cillian's mind went blank, a complete, total whiteout as he shot against the wall and his belly with a soft cry.

He surfaced seconds later but couldn't have said his own name if asked. He braced himself against the wall with his arm, rested his forehead there as he fought simply to breathe. The orgasm had torn through him, leaving his body unsettled, his mind barely registering that the rough man was cleaning off his stomach and cock. Pulling his pants up for him. Taking care of him, which left Cillian feeling odd. Odder still that he liked it.

Cillian had been mauled and licked and bitten, and he'd see—*feel*—the marks for days to come. That was the price of this kind of sex. And he was gladly prepared to pay.

A final bite and then the heat of the broad body left Cillian's back, and he knew without turning around that the man was gone.

Gone, and leaving Cillian wanting more. He debated hunting the man down, turning the tables, but he suspected that still wouldn't be enough. And then what else would they do? Exchange phone numbers? That didn't happen, not in these clubs or in his line of work.

He pushed away from the wall and headed for the exit, satiated but still needy. As he walked through the room and into the bar, his eyes finally adjusted to the dark, he noticed the way the other men were glancing at him. Must've been quite a show, which meant he must look well fucked—a *good* look for him. Several men came on quite strongly, blatantly brushing their bodies against his, asking to buy him drinks . . . one even trying to guide him into the back room again, asking if he wanted to do it again.

He did, but not with any of them.

Just as he was about to leave for the night, a commotion started along the outer part of the dance floor. Chairs went flying, beer bottles and glasses broke, men were shouting, and suddenly it seemed like everyone in the club was involved in the fight. The bouncers circled, trying to figure out where exactly to dive into the fray, and Cillian was sure the police would arrive soon. He wondered if his man from the back room was involved somehow and decided it was better he didn't know.

He rubbed his face where a scratchy cheek had rubbed his raw. His neck and shoulder burned from the bites, his dick ached, although his ass ached worse, and he'd never been more relaxed in his entire life.

But on his way out, something—someone—made him stop and double back to stare into the crowd. He couldn't find the man he thought he'd seen again, but that fleeting glance brought all of his tension back with a vengeance.

Prophet.

CHAPTER TWO

Mal punched a few guys on the way out of the brawl, his adrenaline still buzzing, sex and violence clinging to him like a red haze he had to fight off to see through.

But it didn't matter how many guys he punched tonight, because he'd still smell like that son of a bitch goddamned spy, the scent stronger than smoke or sweat or whiskey. Fucking Cillian had seemed like a good idea at the time, but it had gotten Mal riled up to the point where the only thing that'd take him back down again was a good, old-fashioned bar fight.

And a fight had been necessary for distraction anyway. Whenever his old SEAL team got together in one place, it broke all kinds of laws—and probably a little bit of the universe besides—and they only risked it when completely necessary. Because all the high-tech secured phone lines and internet connections in the world couldn't beat a good old face-to-face meeting.

All that, and it was just midnight.

Now, he slid easily through the crowded streets of the teeming city and headed to his hotel. His, and Cillian's.

His phone soon beeped with the check-in texts—Prophet, then King and Ren, and finally Hook—indicating they were all clear. He added his own confirmation. He'd get an encrypted message soon regarding what they'd be doing next, based on their discussion.

But he hadn't been involved in the discussion portion of the meeting. That hadn't been the plan, but rather, the way things shook out. Mal had spied his alternate job just as his team gathered in the club. He'd known Cillian was in Amsterdam, of course—his team had met here precisely because he was following the damned man, and this was where the damned man was based at the moment. But hell, of all the gay discos in all the world . . .

Rather than let Cillian notice Prophet, or any of the others, Mal had made the executive decision to distract the spy. And ended up distracting the hell out of himself.

Motherfucking shit.

Once he reached his hotel, he moved through the lobby cautiously, took the stairs to the fourth floor and checked his room for any disturbances before he let himself relax. He ordered room service via text to the hotel kitchen—an inroad he'd learned to make early on after losing the ability to speak, because his job also necessitated living in too many hotels to count over the past three years—and then stretched out on the bed. It was time to capitalize on what had happened tonight with Cillian. He grabbed his laptop and scanned all of Prophet's emails, easily blowing a couple of password-protected things and then hitting one that he couldn't get through. A message popped up from Proph—a message with a picture of Mal giving the finger.

Fucker. Like that wouldn't egg him on? He was just about to get serious when he caught sight of Proph's IM contacts—and just the name he'd been looking for—along with the security system information Proph promised him. The last piece of the puzzle that Mal hadn't tried to get on his own, for fear of tipping Cillian off. Hell, he had some respect for the man's abilities.

Now, he logged in to Prophet's home computer so he could access the man's alarm codes, the encryption bouncing back to register him in Prophet's apartment. Which meant he also had access to just about all of Prophet's email and other files. And yeah, when you lived and died for someone, you were allowed to invade their browser history without question or recrimination.

Mal worried about neither. Ah hell, they had no secrets between them anyway. Even if Proph tried—like when he'd *tried* to pretend he wasn't falling for Tom—it didn't work.

And apparently, Cillian hadn't wanted Prophet to have secrets either, since he'd moved into Prophet's building three years earlier, taking over the bottom two floors of the industrial building that had been converted into two apartments.

Prophet had known the guy was a spook from the start, but it wasn't until last year, when Cillian had actively saved Prophet from a kidnapping, that they'd realized how much of Cillian's concern was related to keeping an eye out for John Morse, their fucking asshole traitor of an ex-teammate who might or might not be alive. Now, all of them, Cillian included, were in a race to find John.

Cillian appeared to have the advantage by being the only one who knew for sure if John was dead or alive. At the very least, Cillian had ties to Sadiq—the terrorist John had joined forces with ten plus years earlier—which was enough of a reason to follow the fuck out of the spook. And the fact that Cillian had agreed to help Prophet track down John—and had subsequently told Prophet that John was most definitely dead when they all suspected he was lying—meant that Cillian was on Mal's shit list.

So it was time to end this shit once and for all. And since Prophet had finally given Mal the nod to move ahead at full force, Mal hadn't looked back once.

So far, Mal had traced Cillian through Jakarta and Indonesia. The guy was good, and Mal always thrived on a challenge. And Mal knew one damned thing for sure—John Morse wasn't dead. He'd bet his life on it.

Then again, he did that every single day he looked for his former teammate.

Mal was going to enjoy taking John down. If he had to pimp himself out to Cillian in order to drag that lying scumbag of a traitor out into the open, he'd do it, because at this point, Mal was pretty well convinced that all roads from Cillian led to John. Since Proph couldn't keep trailing John without Cillian on his ass, Mal had taken Cillian's ass into his own hands.

Literally.

Shit.

He blinked and hardened thinking about the spy's dark-haired handsomeness, the British accent that hit the right notes along his cock, and yeah, it was always better when a job was fun.

He'd done his homework on Cillian, but after tonight's first contact, he was now intent on finding out who Cillian—not Cillian-the-spook—really was.

It was kind of like the game Two Truths and a Lie. Most spooks always added elements of truth to their cover, so they didn't end up blowing things when their natural inclinations showed through.

He'd seen Cillian fuck his way through many nights—ninety-nine percent of the time, the guy topped. He'd also watched Cillian in D/s clubs twice—both times, he went for the subs. And while Cillian hadn't fought Mal off tonight, being fucked wasn't something that came easily to the spook. Mal figured the Dom thing was probably a truth.

Now, he looked through Proph's IM history. Apparently, Proph and Cillian had been in contact since nearly the first week the spook had moved in and wired the entire place from top to bottom. Of course, this gave Cillian the ability to track Prophet's entire apartment, but he'd given as good as he'd gotten, which meant Prophet could do exactly the same. And both men could lock the other out for as long as they wished. But hell, in their business, it was always good to have someone watching your place for other enemies. Because even enemies could sometimes be friends.

That alarm system was coming in handy now—for Mal, anyway.

Pages and pages of IMs with Cillian that sounded a lot like Prophet talking to any of his teammates—sarcasm, general assholishness, straightforward flirting. But no actual sexting. Plenty of goddamned talk about it, though, in the way that only two men who were used to being covert could be.

Mal would've asked Cillian if he wanted to fuck goddamned nine hundred texts earlier.

And that fucking couch. Mal made a mental note to throw the thing out of Prophet's window, blowing it up like a Molotov cocktail on the way down.

For the love of fuck, did either of them stop to think that they could've done the entire *Kama Sutra* at this point? All talk and no sex meant that the attraction between these guys was something neither of them wanted to act on. Whatever the reason, Mal was glad they hadn't.

Only because it might've fucked with his plan, of course. Not that he was jealous or anything.

But it'd been a hell of a long time since anyone had flirted with him like this. Probably had something to do with the fact that he told most people to fuck off before any of them could get close enough. Prophet had let Cillian in a little—and Cillian had returned the favor—but that's because it was easy.

Tom, on the other hand, had been the opposite of easy for Prophet. And look where they were now. And when the hell had he turned into a psychotherapist?

He could just hear Prophet telling him, *Got the psycho part right*.

After seeing these IM logs, there was no denying that Cillian wanted to fuck Prophet. In fact, thinking about it, Mal was downright insulted that Cillian might've been thinking about Prophet while Mal had been fucking him. Because that was completely unacceptable, and it left Mal determined to leave his own mark.

Well, more of them anyway.

He smiled at that, and smiled more when he realized that Cillian's flirting with Prophet had to chap Tom's ass. He made a mental note to break into Tom's computer, for the hell of it. After he turned Cillian's world upside-fucking-down.

He grabbed his iPad and hit a contact. When his call was answered, he typed, *Did you fuck him?*

Tom Boudreaux glared at him from the screen. "Who?"

Cillian.

Tom sighed, obviously exasperated. "First of all, you know I'm not Prophet—you're staring right the fuck at me, Mal."

Mal smiled, typed, *Wanted you to ask him for me,* and watched Tom's face redden with anger. Again.

"I'm not asking him that."

Why? You want to know, don't you?

"I fucking hate you."

Perfect. My plan worked. Now, answer the question—was there any contact between Prophet and Cillian that involved tongue. Or cock?

"I'm not answering shit," Tom growled, and Mal caught sight of Prophet in the background of the iPad's screen, walking closer to Tom and shaking his head. Tom mumbled, and there was jostling, and then Prophet's face appeared on screen, with Tom hanging over his shoulder.

"Why you gotta do that, Mal?" Proph asked him.

I like causing strife and chaos. Think of me as the anti-Claus.

"More like the Antichrist," Tom called out, and Mal had to grudgingly admit that wasn't bad at all.

Now you're beginning to understand. Will someone answer the question, because this is fucking important.

Prophet gave *him* the finger this time and cut the call, and Mal took that as *we came close, but it never happened.* Prophet liked keeping Tom slightly jealous because that shit made for hot-as-hell sex.

But wait for it . . .

Three.

Two.

One . . .

The screen flickered back on, and Prophet demanded, "Hold on a minute, did *you* fuck him?"

Mal just smiled, and in the background, Tom hooted right before Mal cut the connection. *Don't say I never did anything for you, you voodoo asshole.*

Now he was ready to take their planning and plotting to the next level. He'd refused to tell Prophet exactly what that next level entailed. No use implicating both of them.

He stood, lowered his pants, and grabbed his phone.

CHAPTER THREE

Cillian stripped the clothes he'd worn to the club, rubbing the bites on his shoulder as he logged on to his computer . . . and found a dick staring him in the face.

He sat back and studied it for a second, because honestly, it was a really good dick, and then he read the note below the picture. Only then did he IM back, *I know that's not you, Prophet.*

The response came back seconds later, still from Prophet's account. *How?*

Because Prophet never sends me pictures of his dick. Nor does he ask for pictures of mine in return.

Who's the idiot in this equation then?

A pause, and then Cillian typed, *You might have a point.*

It wasn't Tom, either. The man didn't have the control over his temper where Cillian was concerned. Maybe he was justified, since Cillian had punched him out last year.

That made Cillian smile. Still, he knew he should get off the computer and not engage with a random friend or colleague of Prophet—not like this, anyway. But he glanced at the picture of the dick again. Long. Thick. Cut. Prominent vein. Hard. And whoever it belonged to was groomed, but not to the point of ridiculousness.

The picture had his attention. Could the actual person keep it?

The man on the other end of the computer wasn't ready to end things, anyway. *So?* appeared in the chat window.

So what? Cillian replied.

Turnabout's fair play.

That's not exactly the right expression for this, but I think you should at least buy me dinner first, Cillian chided.

Too much work. Just show me your cock.

And then what?

Are you always this difficult?

Actually, yes.

Figures. You're definitely a friend of Prophet's.

Are you? Cillian asked. He was surprised that Prophet allowed his computer to be accessed so easily, but then again, sometimes leaving certain things easily accessed stopped people from looking for other things too hard. Locking everything down could actually create more risk.

Words appeared in the IM window. *More like a favor than a friend.*

Cillian slid his fingertips along the smooth surface of the laptop, just below the keys. IMing with Prophet was easy, mainly because, as much and as often as they'd flirted, neither of them actually seemed to think anything else would happen between them. And that had been true even before Tom came into the picture. Cillian had held back as much as Prophet had and no doubt for the same reason.

As operatives went, Prophet was ahead of the curve. In fact, he'd been considered something of a wunderkind. Cillian knew all about that, having been something of a wunderkind himself. It happened enough in this community: men like them thrived in adverse conditions like this, especially once they were allowed to use their skills instead of fighting their natural leadership—and asshole—tendencies. They shined. So it was no surprise they were all drawn to each other and that sense of community that constantly challenged them. Because the only one who could challenge another crazy was one of their kind . . .

But dating another operative? Never. A complete and utter disaster. Which is why Prophet dating Tom still surprised Cillian. Prophet had to know his relationship with Tom could implode.

Speaking of imploding, Cillian considered his new—and slightly demanding—IM buddy. Chatting with this guy wasn't unlike the opening moves of a chess match and that intrigued him a bit more than he'd like to admit. He told himself it was because he could simply practice his more subtle interrogation skills while hidden behind a screen.

After waiting several seconds and staring at a blank response box, he finally typed, *So, who are you?*

I showed you my dick and you're concerned about my name?

Yes.

Now you've insulted me.

Somehow, I think it would take more than that. It's a nice cock, though.

Nice? Fuck off.

Cillian smiled in spite of himself. *So why are you staying with Prophet?*

He owes my father a favor.

That sounded right on Prophet's end. *Are you sending dick pictures to all of Prophet's contacts?*

You're the only one I found.

Cillian cut the contact off and texted Prophet. *I've been chatting with your houseguest.*

Seconds later, Prophet texted back. *Ah shit, I told Mal he could use my computer to check his emails. I didn't know he'd use my IM. Don't worry, the alarm stuff isn't accessible.*

I figured as much. And location services was pinpointing Prophet as somewhere near the apartment, which meant he was in New York, not Amsterdam. Cillian shook off the image he thought he'd seen at the club, chalked it up to being all wound up from the back-room sex.

Is he bothering you?

Cillian smiled. *He sent me a picture of his dick.*

Ah Christ, the guy's a pain in my ass.

Literally? What does Tom have to say about that?

He'd have plenty to say to you about that, Cillian. Cut it the fuck out.

Prophet's new partner had come into the picture at a most unfortunate time, just as Cillian was insinuating himself into Prophet's life. Still, Cillian had gained enough of Prophet's trust for Prophet to confide in him about his search for his missing teammate and ex-lover. And more importantly, to ask for his help.

Since Morse had sold out his SEAL team, his country, and his best friend and lover, Prophet Drews, Cillian had been charged with shadowing Prophet in addition to tracking—perhaps as a way *to* track—John. Although he'd seen no direct signs that the men were in contact, he had no doubt that John was behind Prophet's kidnapping last year.

Like Cillian, Prophet Drews and his teammates had attempted to track John for years. But Cillian wasn't working for or with them. He worked for SB-20, a mysterious organization in its own right, cloak and dagger, completely classified, all just the way Cillian preferred it. And the information—the lie—Cillian had told Prophet about John being dead was exactly what the CIA had in their files. Prophet would be an idiot to believe him fully, and the man was no idiot . . . but the seeds of doubt had been planted.

And Cillian liked Prophet too much to not plant those seeds, because he knew one thing for sure—Prophet would pull John and their former team right out into the open. Whether or not that was a good thing . . .

Well, good for whom was the real question.

But the bottom line was that Cillian had to be the one to kill John. Whatever he needed to do to ensure that happened, including keeping Prophet away, he'd do it. And he'd already had to keep both Prophet and his boyfriend away. Tom was experienced in some ways, but he was relatively new to the intrigue of the spy game, and his attempts last year to help Prophet, to try to stop him from self-destructing, had forced Cillian into the game in person.

Speaking of Tom, have you seen your boyfriend lately? Because I have. He could practically hear Prophet bitching and muttering under his breath. *Call him off, Prophet.*

I did.

Then you need a stronger chain, because he's chewing through the leash. And tell me more about your houseguest.

Didn't realize I needed to give you an itinerary every time someone sleeps over.

Are there that many of them?

Jesus Christ, Cillian, you're lucky Tom isn't here reading this. I swear you do it just to get me in trouble.

Cillian felt the slightest tingle of jealousy, except this time, it was more about realizing that Prophet would soon not be available to chat at a moment's notice—already, there were days when Prophet turned off the computer and the alarm system on his end entirely. Cillian loved the chase almost as much as he loved pushing Prophet's buttons. In fact, he'd taken it as a personal challenge every time they were online together. But it was increasingly obvious that the man was solidly taken, if the way he looked at Tom was any indication. And that disappointed Cillian far more than he'd cared to admit, but mainly because he was used to getting and having his own way with the men of his choice.

Cillian could only assume Prophet hadn't pulled Mal off the computer because Mal, for whatever reason he was really with Prophet, would be a good distraction for Cillian. *So you've taken in a drifter? Really, Prophet?*

He swore he could feel Prophet's eye roll through the phone. *The guy's all fucked up. He developed some kind of software, sold his company but kept his shares. He's loaded, smart, and bored as fuck—the worst possible combination. But he's harmless. I just did a job with his dad and sister. Didn't know the kid existed until she called and asked for a favor.*

So you provide day care now?

Are they showing dick pictures in day care these days?

Point taken.

If there was one thing he identified with Prophet, it was guilt, and that man had it in spades. So he assured Prophet, *It's all right. He seems like an okay kid.*

He's a juvenile delinquent hiding in a man's body. He's also lost. Aren't we all?

And just when I didn't think you had a heart.

Cillian let him have the last word. Or let Prophet think he had, anyway, because Cillian was already texting his supervisor. A few keystrokes and he was checking Prophet's story regarding Mal. Of course, there wouldn't be much, a skeleton file among skeleton files, if anything. But in his business, you could never be too careful, too paranoid . . . or take too many chances.

The ultimate paradox.

CHAPTER FOUR

Mal sat back to wait for Cillian to do his fact-checking. Prophet texted him about his contact with Cillian, which meant that, if all went according to plan, Cillian would be running Mal's alias through his handlers.

People thought the spy shit, like building an alias, was easy, which is why they sucked at it. There were layers of intricacy to the setup that the average person never even considered. Mal was used to a million different identities. Juggling the different facets of his life, the majority of which included fucking with his family and hunting down John Morse, was a necessary evil, and one he did extremely well.

He enjoyed the games. Otherwise, he'd be drifting aimlessly. And although he'd like to be in the same room with his team whenever he felt like it, that wouldn't happen until he pulled this off.

For three months, he'd followed Cillian. Planning. Stalking. Waiting. And now, preparation had just given opportunity a handjob. The plan he and Prophet worked on last month was about to execute, and once it did, all the balls were back in Mal's court.

He almost jumped out of his skin when the phone at the other side of his bed rang. Fucking, fucking King and his insistence on having five million devices. He pulled up the FaceTime program and mouthed, *What the fuck, King?*

King's eyes narrowed. "Good choice of words. Your spook stayed in the back room just long enough for us to finish. Quite a coincidence, young Mal."

Fuck off, King.

King's heavy brogue came through on the subsequent laugh. "We took bets on it—me, Ren, and Hook."

Who won?

"Hook."

Of course.

"You're being careful, lad?"

King was the only guy in the world Mal'd let get away with that *lad* shit. He allowed it because King meant it . . . because it meant so much to both of them. In their language, it was the most comforting thing they could say. *Trying to*, he mouthed.

"Say the word, Mal, and I'm there to take this part on."

King was already as far from Amsterdam as he could get in a few hours—Mal was certain of that. Which meant Ren was as well, with Hook having gone in the opposite direction, hemming John in, circling the man's last known location so they could tighten like a noose. But now his throat tightened instead as he realized he hated having missed the meeting, because he missed the fuck out of his teammates. Even though one call would have them in this room at a moment's notice, he wouldn't do that and risk putting them in more danger than they already were.

He ignored King's request, instead mouthing, *Anything else?*

"Sent the intel you requested through to your spook's informant regarding your aliases."

Because Cillian knew all of Prophet's team, except for Mal's real identity. Mal was certain Cillian had never been able to get a bead on the man he referred to as the "missing teammate," because, thanks to the power of WITSEC, Mal had enlisted in the Navy under an alias. Even the Feds couldn't access that shit, and even if and when they did, Seamus Dwyer and SO2 Colton Miller were both long buried. Finding out who he'd been in the past would prove to be a bitch.

Mal was the real thorn in Cillian's side. Now, he was about to prove it.

And finally, he answered King's earlier question. *I'm fine. I'll see this through.*

"Never doubted you for a minute," King said quietly, before hanging up.

His main phone buzzed, the hotel's concierge letting him know that his food was on the way and asking if he needed anything else that evening. Since what he needed was staying a few floors below in the same hotel, he texted back a *no thanks*.

He rubbed his throat as he typed, could hear his voice in his mind—that strong, Southie Boston accent—whenever he typed or signed and especially when he mouthed words. Mob Irish, born and (then) bred, just not in the same place.

Mob Irish, just like King, although King's mob ties were across the pond and deep into post-IRA Sinn Féin territory. Mortal enemies, placed on the same team. Because the universe was that fucked up.

"Shoulda feckin' been me," King had said the night Mal's throat had been cut, in a brogue that was as heavy as the narcotic pain meds they'd snowed Mal with. King had come to the States when he was fifteen, but because his mom was American, he'd always had citizenship. He could erase his brogue when he needed to, but it came out heavily under provocation. Didn't happen often, but after Mal's throat was cut, he was the angriest Mal had ever seen him.

He'd known he'd been slashed deeply, but learning he wasn't able to talk . . . well fuck, he'd never considered that he might never be able to speak again. King had broken the news, blunt as always, and Mal, stubborn as always, tried every fucking way he could think of to talk.

Hadn't happened yet. Vocal cord damage was a bitch, and the surgery that had saved his life had contributed to that loss. He was lucky he'd lived, and hell, he didn't need a voice to do the things he did. Didn't need a conscience either, but like Proph said, you couldn't shred the fucker as easily as vocal cords.

But even Proph had to admit that Mal had come damned close. And Mal wanted it to stay that way. Needed it to. Needed to figure out once and for all if their former teammate-turned-possible-terrorist, John Morse, was the one who'd cut his goddamned throat . . . and if he was the one behind the most recent attempt on Prophet's life.

I'll get you, you fucker, he mouthed, hearing the barest hint of sound. Unintelligible, of course. He'd been seeing a specialist, an ENT who'd been giving him experimental injections, and he'd told Mal about an operation—a graft—that might help him. It might also make things worse, and at best, it meant months of recovery and rehab, but at the moment, Mal wasn't ready to give up his best chance of putting this chapter of their lives solidly behind them.

CHAPTER FIVE

The fact-checkers at SB-20 got back to Cillian within five minutes. The intel on Prophet's last job was only available because he'd been working black ops. If it had been done for the CIA, there would be no trace of it. But even though the Agency had requisitioned the job through a private contractor, they were all CYA by leaving Prophet's mission unclassified—there if you knew what to look for, but not easily available for any passing terrorist. Inexplicable fucking bureaucracies. But at least it was working in his favor this time.

His handler, Trent, typed the intel. *Prophet's last black ops job was rescuing a girl named Kasey Coetzee. I've got a home number for her and a cell for her brother Mal.*

Cillian didn't bother responding, dialed the home number for somewhere in Middle America, and when a woman picked up, he said, "I'm looking for Mal Coetzee."

"He's not here. Can I take a message?" Even as Cillian was about to tell her not to bother, she continued, "Wait, is this about the job offer? Because he's in New York at the moment, but I know he's been waiting to hear. He's willing to relocate."

Cillian nodded into the phone at the corroboration. "I guess I mixed up the house and cell numbers. I'll give him a call on his cell phone then, yes?" He rattled off the number and she confirmed it with a, "Yes, that's it."

"Perfect. Thank you."

He hung up and stared at the blinking cursor. The IM box showed Prophet—or in this case, Mal—as still logged on. But before he could do anything, his phone buzzed, and he glanced at the number.

Shelby, the missing informant. "I heard you were dead," Cillian said dryly instead of hello.

"Sometimes a man just needs a little space," Shelby told him.

"Things okay?"

"Following a lead."

"That means good things for me, I hope?"

"I'm hoping. Can you meet me tomorrow night? I should have the intel I need by then."

"Yes. Midnight. I'll get you the coordinates half an hour before. I'm assuming you're close by?"

"Yes. I'll wait for the text, and I'll be there," Shelby promised.

As Cillian hung up, he stared again at the blinking cursor on the IM screen. He stopped worrying and typed, *Are you going to tell me your name?*

Whatever. It's Mal. Who are *you* Cillian? What's your deal?

And here I thought you were only interested in my dick. I'm just Prophet's neighbor.

Dude, I'm not an operative, but I'm also not stupid.

No, I'm guessing you're anything but.

You definitely checked me out with Prophet. Because that last comment's a nice, subtle way of giving me the whole "You're a smart guy, so why are you bumming around?" lecture.

Even though Mal was projecting on that last part, Cillian couldn't deny it. Instead, he asked, *Did he scold you for IMing me?*

He tried.

Cillian sighed. *I told him not to.*

S'all right. Think I can't deal with him?

Can you?

I'm still on his computer, aren't I?

You're also a brat.

You have no idea, Cillian. There was a pause, and then, *But do you want to?*

The last thing he'd expected to do tonight was get fucked, and then meet a brat who tried to seduce him.

Mal wasn't stupid. He apparently knew more about the possibilities Cillian's jobs might entail than any man he'd dated in the past. That alone made him dangerous. The dick pic was just icing on the cake.

Besides, a computer screen was far more controllable than real life. He'd had several relationships like this, although usually after an initial real-life meeting.

But he'd never much believed in rules. Not when it came to fucking, anyway, and because of that, Cillian refused to say no. Instead, he simply responded, *Let's see where the conversation takes us.*

Are you as fucked up as Prophet?

Are you?

For sure.

Cillian pushed it. *In what way?*

I need to find myself.

Liar. Why no military?

Stole cars when I was younger. In several states and countries. We moved around too often for me to do much in school.

Cillian knew there were ways around the arrest record if Mal had truly wanted to go into the military. But the man had found other ways to keep busy. *So what are you doing now?*

Besides freeloading off Prophet?

Yes, besides that.

I can hear your sarcasm from here, BTW.

We both know you're not exactly a couch surfer. Or, rather, you don't need to be.

True. I could buy this entire place. Want me to make an offer?

I'm happy with my residence, so no. Answer the question. You've made money. What's next? Pray it lasts forever?

Oh, there's the lecture. And I'm probably going out to LA. Got a friend who can give me a job bouncing at a couple of clubs. Good money, hours I like. Don't have to think for a while.

And no future.

That's sweet that I show you my dick and you're worried about my future.

Sweet isn't how I'd describe myself, Mal. If you ever met me in person, I'd show you that.

There was a pause—long enough for Cillian to know that Mal was seriously considering his words, and then Mal typed, *Why can't you show me here anyway?*

It was Cillian's turn to pause. Finally, he typed, *I don't know you well enough to spoil you.*

The man on the other end of the screen sent him a picture of his hand this time, and strangely enough, Mal giving him the finger made Cillian want to get to know him better.

Tapped into Prophet's texts, Mal had waited patiently while Cillian contacted Prophet about him, watched with a smile as Prophet played Cillian like a fucking violin. Kasey had given the all clear a bit later, and to cement his story as her brother, Mal had fed the intel they'd created into the computer so Cillian and whoever his people were could find it.

But now, he only waited a few seconds after sending his trademark snapshot before engaging with Cillian again. *What if I spoiled you, Cillian?*

And just how do you plan on doing that?

Mal closed his eyes for a second, remembering Cillian's body against his, how the man responded to the rough play. Mal knew enough to recognize that Cillian hadn't been completely at ease giving up control. Some of that would have to do with being a spook, but a big part of it was simply his sexual wiring . . . the man was definitely more of a dominant. *Any way I want to. I think you'd like letting it be my choice.*

There was a pause, and then Cillian told him, *I think you don't know me.*

Bullshit I don't, Mal mouthed, then typed, *I know I'd have you any way I wanted you.*

You're very confident.

You like that, right? Want someone who's confident enough to just slam you down and take you, just because they can?

Doesn't everyone have that fantasy every now and again?

Mal's dick hardened. *Yeah, so if I was in control (which I am), what would you want me to do? Push you against the wall?*

Again, his thoughts returned to the back room of the club . . . figured Cillian was doing the same. Especially when Cillian responded, *I'd let you maul me. Bite me, suck on me . . .*

Can I leave marks?

He pictured Cillian's hand, trailing over the marks Mal had left on his skin. Mal knew from experience they'd still be aching, that Cillian would be feeling him all over, for days.

Cillian finally typed, *Yes.*

Good. Because I'm pushing you down on your knees. You're going to suck me until *I* come. And if it's good enough, I might let *you* come. If not . . . you're not touching yourself, are you, Cillian?

No.

Then get my pants down and take me in your mouth. Mal unzipped his pants and started stroking his cock as he unrolled the fantasy.

There was another pause before Cillian typed, *I'm taking your zipper down with my teeth. Shoving your pants down, and then I'm taking your cock in deep, swallowing it, making you curse. You're cursing me, yes?*

Oh yeah, Cillian was getting into it. *Yes. And I've got a grip on your hair. A tight one.*

Want me to stop?

Fuck you. And no.

I wouldn't, even if you asked. Because I'm going to make you lose the control you're trying so hard to hang on to. Because you're barely hanging on, right?

Fuck. Mal palmed his cock, trying not to respond to Cillian in any way that would show that he was losing control. *Just keep using your mouth where I want it.*

Don't worry about me. I'm stroking underneath your balls now. While I'm sucking. And before you can stop me, I've pulled you forward, and I've got a finger in your ass, and you're barely able to stand up. But you are, because I'm not giving you the option. Your hands are digging into my shoulders now, and you're balancing yourself. People are watching you . . . starting to gather around.

Mal stared at the screen, stroking his cock faster. He wanted to type some more orders, but couldn't understand how the fuck he'd lost control so easily.

After I make you come in my mouth, I'm going to take you over my knee, right in front of everyone. And you're going to love it.

Fuck. Mal came all over his hands, his stomach . . . his mouth forming a silent howl as his body jerked. He closed his eyes and then opened them quickly, hoping he could salvage this. And wondering if it mattered.

You came, Cillian typed.

No.

You paused. Which means you're lying.

Mal huffed, thinking, *Means I'm trying to wipe up the cum,* but he typed one-handed, *You're going to have to do better than that if you want me to come.*

Are you lying because you need a spanking? Or because you're a brat and can't help yourself?

Mal got hard again in his hand. He hissed and stared at the screen, pissed he'd lost this round, but realizing he'd needed this so damned badly. It'd been too long since he'd submitted. And while he most preferred the dominant role, there was something to be said about pulling that switch, especially when it hit his masochistic buttons. He wouldn't fuck any of the people he trusted with his life, although those trusted ones did help him quite a bit, since it was too hard to give himself over to just anyone.

But hiding behind the screen wasn't too hard. At least not yet.

CHAPTER SIX

Twenty-four hours later, Cillian was about to leave for his meeting with Shelby when the phone started ringing.

Speak of the devil. Half an hour before, he'd texted the man the coordinates to the alley behind the Forestor Hotel. Now, Cillian picked up on the first ring, not bothering to couch the warning in his tone. "If you're canceling—"

He was stopped by a stuttered breath that sounded suspiciously like Shelby was being held by the throat. And even though he should hang up and cut his losses—his job was about profit and loss, after all—he couldn't. Because he understood Prophet and his guilt more than he cared to admit. "Shelby, what's going on?"

Another strangled sound greeted him, and Cillian cursed and left the room. He took the stairs so the phone wouldn't cut out, and finally, as he hit the lobby, Shelby tried to answer.

His voice was still choked, and Cillian had to ask Shelby to repeat himself three times before he could make out, "He said I had to call."

Cillian walked quickly down the street. "Shelby, who are you talking about?" There were too many *he*s in Cillian's life for that to be even remotely clear. "Put whoever's with you on the phone. I can pay," he lied, but it did no good.

"He said to tell you that he knows the plan. And he knows the truth."

And then the click of a gun—the sound of the trigger being pulled back close to the phone—echoed in Cillian's ear.

"He says . . ." Shelby's voice shook with a fear so palpable, Cillian swore he could smell it over the phone. "He says I need to tell you good-bye."

It was like Shelby was reading from a cue card. Cillian couldn't hear any other sound but Shelby's breathing. Like the man was alone.

There was a single gunshot—deafening over the phone and taking a split second longer to register in real life. It sounded like a firecracker, so it must have been fired through a silencer. Cillian remained on the open line until he realized the fear he smelled was his. That jolted him into immediate action, and he hung up, in case whoever had shot Shelby was trying to trace the call. He was bouncing the signal, but you couldn't be too careful.

He approached the familiar alleyway carefully, weapon drawn before he rounded the corner. As a meeting place, it was normally safe and quiet, but now it was only the latter—at least for Shelby, who was lying facedown on the concrete, blood pooling under his head and expanding in a dark river away from him.

Cillian went up and down the alleyway first, checking doors and windows, and the street—and he saw no one, heard nothing beyond the familiar clank and shouts from the kitchen staff of the hotel.

He doubled back and put two fingers against Shelby's neck, but there was no pulse. He checked around the alley again, checked the doors of the buildings that buffered the alley, but they were all locked tight. He looked in the windows and saw nothing but the usual abandoned warehouses he normally saw.

No footprints had been left behind, and Shelby's wallet was gone, but his phone was still in his pocket. No sign of any weapon.

He pocketed the phone, sifted through the rest of Shelby's pockets and came up empty. He left the body, because there was nothing more he could do. As far as he knew, Shelby had no family, so no one would miss him except men like Cillian.

At first glance, Shelby's death could simply mean the informant had screwed over the wrong person, rather than it being a carefully calculated message to Cillian. Informants typically worked for multiple spooks, and they were poached—and killed—all the time.

That still didn't mean he wasn't cautious. He took the long route back to the hotel, but no one followed. Once back in his room, he searched it carefully, texted Trent, and waited for the call back on the secure line.

"Do you think John Morse killed him?" Trent asked after Cillian explained what had happened.

"It's on the list of possibilities, but I can't see him deigning to kill an informant who isn't actually informing me of shit." Cillian ran a hand through his hair. "And what plan? What truth? I'm the only number listed on his phone."

"Dock it anyway," Trent instructed. After a few minutes of furious typing on the other end of the line, he gave a frustrated, "Negative on any other calls but that last one to you. Where was Shelby the last time you contacted him?"

"Indonesia. That was last month. He came to Amsterdam to meet me." The docked phone dinged. "There's a text coming through. Coordinates."

"I see them," Trent said as Cillian watched a picture of Shelby come through next . . . with Cillian crouched next to him, feeling for a pulse, and seeming to stare directly into the camera.

Asshole had been on the roof across the street. Had to be, based on the angle.

"Coordinates are pointing to Ali-Sabieh," Trent said.

"Morse's last known location." Cillian pulled up the photo Karl had shown him last night, a shadowed Morse coming out of a doorway. Impossible to tell where that was taken, but when Trent ran the coordinates and pulled up the location, it looked like a perfect match.

They waited to see if anything more came in, but nothing. Cillian ran the options through his mind: he could go back to the building across the way, he could head to Shelby's hotel room . . . or he could let this go and see what happened next.

As if reading his mind, Trent said, "I'll send someone to his hotel room to check it out."

"Do it fast," Cillian told him.

"Your other informants?"

"Alive and well, as of last check-in. Karl told me that Tom is still following me."

"And you didn't notice?"

"Fuck off, Trent. I made him early and sent him on a wild-goose chase. And he didn't kill my informant. Prophet might have, though, if he doesn't believe me about John."

"Do you think he does?" Trent asked.

"My instinct is no, but he wants to believe something. I figured handing him the best option might help him give up the ghost."

"Maybe lying to him isn't the way to go."

"And maybe it's my fucking op, Trent," Cillian snarled. He'd always showed his supervisor the utmost respect, but this job had been his baby from the start. No one was telling him what to do with it.

He cut the line and hesitated briefly before IMing Mal. To check on Prophet. Granted, he could text Prophet . . . but the thought of talking to Mal made him feel better. And he really needed to feel better right now. *Is Prophet there?*

Why? My dick's not enough?

Cillian snorted. *More than, I suspect.*

Nothing suspect about it. But Prophet's out for the night.

With Tom?

That boyfriend of his? He's away.

Cillian nodded to himself, because at least that fit. He logged in to his personal alarm system and scanned his apartment. All seemed quiet. Then he logged in to Prophet's and found it blocked. Perhaps Prophet had done so to keep his charge from getting into trouble—or to spare Cillian from having to see what kind of trouble he was up to. Prophet tended to block the system more often lately, and Cillian figured that was Tom's doing. But Cillian was no voyeur. When he caught sight of the two men together, he quickly turned the security cams off, because watching them fuck on his couch was not on his to do list.

Mal, however, was on the to do list, even if only virtually. Especially when his next IM appeared. *Touch yourself.*

Cillian raised an eyebrow at the screen. *Who says you get to give the orders?*

Well, you're not.

Cillian's cock hardened, and he found his hand there. *Touch yourself, Mal.*

There was a pause and then . . . *Fuck. Yeah.*

Cillian stroked his own cock and, since he didn't know what Mal looked like, imagined him as the guy who'd fucked him at the club, imagined that guy sitting at his feet, behaving for him. Imagined pinning him to the wall of that back room.

You'd better be doing exactly what I tell you to, he instructed, and was greeted with a hastily typed lowercase *yes.*

Good. Stroke yourself hard, Mal. And tell me to fuck you. Out loud. Pretend I can hear it.

yes

Cillian's breath caught in his throat. He wanted to tell Mal to turn on Skype, wanted to see him come. But the fantasy was better.

The fantasy was always better.

The ringing phone woke him. Cillian had only gotten an hour's sleep, because after his online jack off session with Mal, he'd gone back to the same club he'd met Karl in. There were plenty of other clubs in the area that catered more directly to Cillian's particular needs, but he ruthlessly ignored them, holding on to the irrational hope of finding again that same dark-haired man who'd fucked him.

He might not have gotten the best look at him, but the eyes, the scent, the touch . . . he'd know the man.

Mal had riled him up. And he'd gone to the club to relieve that tension, hoping if he bled it off, he could think straight. When he hadn't found the dark-haired man, he'd fucked some bodybuilder type into submission instead. Then he'd come back, and he'd told Mal what he'd done. And he'd logged off before Mal had a chance to respond.

He rolled over and looked at the name on the phone's screen before accepting the call. "Yes, Peter?"

"Don't be like that, Cillian. I'm on my way." Peter Jenks, petulant asshole on his best day.

"You're also later than you promised."

"Intel doesn't stick to a goddamned fucking schedule. And I don't need your shit."

The hostility was nothing new—from day one, Peter had seemed to resent the fact that an informant was actually expected to produce information. But he was the stepson of some very wealthy and connected men in Albania, and as such, he had access to intel that had helped Cillian over the years.

When Peter first contacted SB-20, it had been because his father had a dinner meeting with Sadiq—and because John had shown up. It had also been because he was facing jail time for smuggling, and he'd known that the information could save him.

"Peter, I'm not in the mood."

"You will be. Meet me for breakfast at ten."

Cillian rolled over and glanced at the clock, and told him, "Make it nine," for no other reason than to retain the control.

CHAPTER SEVEN

Mal had been nine the first time he'd watched someone die.

Back then, someone was always dying—there were wakes held in family living rooms in his community every other day, it seemed. An Irish-Catholic tradition. But paying respects to a dead man laid out in a coffin was really freaking different from watching one bleed out on your back porch.

On that day, he'd cut the last hour of school. Had known he'd catch hell for it, but he caught hell on a regular basis and had figured that he might as well do something to deserve it.

There was no point in being an angel—that lesson had been drilled into him early and often. Hey, the Bible hadn't been his first choice of reading material, but once foisted on him, he twisted it to his advantage. According to the Good Book, angels got the short end of the stick. Lots of work for very little recognition.

But everyone knew Satan.

When he'd brought that up to his religion teacher, he'd gotten his knuckles rapped so hard two had broken. They still ached to this day.

He rubbed them absently now under the warm spray of the shower, swore he could still smell the stewed cabbage leaking out Mrs. O'Malley's window, the sour scent mingling with the garbage as he cut through the alley to sneak into his house.

The argument floated through the still air, stopped Mal just short of rounding the corner to his house. Instead, he flattened against the brick wall of the apartment building and peeked around toward his house.

His dad and Jimmy Finn were standing on the porch, both men gesturing with their hands and talking over each other. Nothing new—his father was always arguing with someone, for sport, for business, over politics or money, and it always ended with a handshake and a beer. Or so Mal had thought until his illusions were shattered as easily as Jimmy's jaw.

After the punch, his father shook his hand out. Jimmy was on the ground in the fetal position, clutching his face, blood dripping from his mouth. Mal's gut clenched when his father circled around behind Jimmy, grabbed Jimmy by the hair, exposing his throat, and slit it.

That trick was a Dwyer family specialty. And no, the irony of that hadn't escaped Mal, sat bitterly on his tongue whenever he revisited that day. He didn't have to close his eyes to see Jimmy Finn lying motionless on the smooth wood where Mal used to run barefoot in the summer, blood spilled where he used to hide out in the coldest winter days so he wouldn't be inside with his father.

It was also ironic that he'd refused to kill for or in the name of his family, had joined the Navy to escape the mob, and had learned how to be a better killer than his family ever could have dreamed. It was like the violence of the world he'd grown up in had embedded itself in him, taken root, and could never be fully excised.

He'd never been able to escape death. Apparently, he was a good Irish Catholic after all.

He shut the water off, rubbed his hair dry with a towel as he walked into the bedroom to scan the internet for anything related to his family, finding the usual articles, a mix of speculation and documented history plus a touch of falsehood that just perpetuated the legends. It had been a slow few months, but that wouldn't last.

Down the hall, someone stirred. Shit like that made living in hotels most of the time a fucking pain in his ass, because he couldn't shut off his hyperawareness. Certain things could quiet it, a certain kind of sex, but lately, he hadn't found anyone he could trust enough to let him indulge.

He stared at the computer screen, specifically at the IM box where Cillian had informed him that he'd gone out and fucked someone, then logged off before Mal could respond. Asshole spook. And who the fuck IMed anymore? Leave it to Prophet to stay old school.

Was that IM business something Cillian did purposely, to get close to Prophet? That thought made Mal's wheels spin, because figuring out the hows and whys of this power play shit had long since stopped being anything but an obsession. Cillian was simply the newest player in the game.

Before he could decide if he would take up with Cillian again tonight, his phone blinked and vibrated. Collect call from an upstate New York prison. Could be several people, but most likely, one of two. And he hoped to hell it wasn't his father.

It wasn't. It was Lucien.

Lucien, with his deep, sarcastic drawl—an Irishman with a Southern accent wasn't exactly the norm, but Lucien had always prided himself on being anything but. "I've been a bad boy, but they gave me one phone call."

You get one phone call a week and you're wasting it on me?

"Never a waste, Seamus." Lucien's voice was graveled and sharp.

Mal typed, *Tell it to the judge.*

"Boy, you need to listen and listen good." Mal knew what was coming—he just hadn't thought Lucien would discover it this fast. "You cannot get involved in this shit."

Too late.

"I realize that."

Did it help?

"You know it did." The short, clipped sentences, the talking about nothing at all while talking about something was a prerequisite of getting information into or out of prison. They could be talking about a fucking fruit basket, because you never knew who the hell would run these tapes and try to stop Lucien's parole, which was coming up fast. "But that's the end."

The end?

"This is the last call, Mal."

Mal's gut tightened. He wanted to ask *why now?*, because he'd certainly fucked up enough before, and Lucien had never, ever cut him off, no matter what. He was the only one who hadn't. But even though Mal's fingers were poised to type the word, they never hit the w-h-y keys. Instead, his forefinger pressed the End Call button, effectively disconnecting him from Lucien's life.

It should be physically harder to do that; instead, a silent, barely pressed button dissolved a lifeline. He shivered—violently—and refused to try making sense of it, because there would never be any. The fact that Lucien hadn't thought he was wasting a call simply meant that cutting someone—Mal being the someone in this instance—out of your life for the good of your family wasn't a waste.

He was right.

Now, Mal typed *Hey* and stared at the computer, waiting for an answer. It was the worst time ever to talk to Cillian—he was off-fucking-balance, not in the driver's seat at all, and logging off was the sensible thing to do.

But Mal never ever did the sensible thing.

CHAPTER EIGHT

Peter looked scared out of his mind, barely able to get the words out as he stared at the screen. "He knows . . . the plan. He knows . . . oh God . . ."

A pause in which Peter bit back a sob, then said, "I can pay."

He said it directly to the camera, like whoever was holding him there by restraints or with threat of a weapon—either impossible to see because Peter was only being shown from the shoulders up—was directly behind the camera. Or holding it.

Finally, Peter said dully, "He knows the truth. And he's going to fucking kill you. And he says . . . he's going to enjoy it."

Cillian forced himself to watch the impact of the throwing knife that pierced Peter's carotid—Peter's eyes opened wide, blood spurted out of his neck—and then the video ended.

It'd come through to Cillian's phone minutes ago, just after he'd returned to his hotel room, fresh from a meeting with a new possible source, someone who claimed to have an inside track to Sadiq. The time stamp was four hours earlier—a full hour after Peter had missed his meeting with Cillian, pissing Cillian off enough to break into Peter's hotel room—nothing had been out of order—and stalk some of Peter's usual haunts. He'd also checked in remotely with Karl and Vince, who were both fine.

Just like he'd assumed Peter had been.

"Shit. *Shit*," he muttered as he buzzed through to Trent, knowing that this pretty much confirmed Shelby's death was related to either himself or to John—or both. The message could be for either of them . . .

"You think it's Prophet?" Trent asked him.

"No," Cillian said as he logged in to the apartment's security system to see Prophet lying on his bed, reading a magazine. The man was good, but there was no way he'd done this in person. A further perusal showed the shadowed profile of a dark-haired man—not Tom—lying on his stomach, staring at a laptop.

Trent was silent, his anger palpable over the phone. And fuck, Cillian was pissed too. He'd also been with SB-20 long enough to know he was only as good as his last job.

"Someone is purposefully hunting down your informants." Trent's words were measured. "What information could've been extracted from Shelby and Peter in regard to their jobs for you?"

"That I'm after John Morse. I haven't exactly made that a goddamned secret." Cillian spoke through clenched teeth. "I'll make sure it's under control."

"You'd better. Two of your best informants dead in less than twenty-four hours. You don't even know what intel Peter was bringing you. I hope your others are well protected. Either that or dangle them as bait." Trent played the video again, and Cillian watched it again until, out of the corner of his eye, he saw Mal's icon—an avatar of his dick pic—pop up on his personal computer. Mal's icon, not Prophet's, with a single message. *Hey.*

That was all. *Hey.* Cillian's fucking informants were dropping like flies, and he had no goddamned time for this *hey* shit.

Still, it didn't stop him from typing back *Hey* as Trent continued to lecture him on the importance of this mission. Like Cillian didn't know that. His mind spun through the wheel of possibilities, even as Mal answered with, *Figured I'd use my own ID.*

Letting me know your email address. Big step. Sure you're ready for that kind of commitment?

I'm pretty sure I want you to shut up and open your ass for me.

"Jesus Christ," he breathed.

"We'll figure it out, Cillian," Trent told him.

Cillian straightened in his chair as his cock stood at full attention. He flicked the keys quietly. *You think I'm that easy.*

Nothing to think about. I know it.

He told his supervisor, "I'm handling it. I've gotten further on this job than anyone else ever could have. It's why you gave it to me. You know that's true."

He'd gotten further than Prophet, even though Prophet had spent two years searching for Morse. Two years of doing nothing but combing the earth with his relentless grief and guilt, according to all the reports Cillian had seen. Meanwhile, Cillian had been in the same goddamned room as Morse—that fucking traitor—so his guilt was on par with Prophet's. Now, Cillian didn't give a shit who was fucking with him. Because he was about to fuck with them back, and it was going to be harder than they ever thought possible.

Tonight you're going over my lap, he told Mal, and there was a long enough pause that he knew Mal was definitely on goddamned board.

Mal didn't answer Cillian's statement. Couldn't, because he was frozen, half-wanting that *going over his lap* thing so fucking badly and half-wanting to run from it. God, this was so fucking stupid. But running, cutting off contact, wouldn't work—not now, anyway.

And he didn't want to cut off comms with Cillian. *Because of the job*, he told himself firmly, and his dick laughed at him.

You're quiet, Cillian finally typed.

Yeah, you can tell after knowing me five whole minutes? Aren't you the psychic? He waited for Cillian to log off, because God knew the guy didn't need to put up with shit from someone he didn't need in his life.

But instead, he said, *It's been longer than five minutes. What can I do?*

Mal gave an openmouthed sigh as he leaned back in his chair. Hesitated, then typed, *Whatever you think's best.*

Words he'd never willingly said to anyone before.

I want you over my lap ... I've told you that. But for the moment, I think you need something stronger.

A tremble rippled through Mal, and he glanced around the room. He was alone. This wasn't real. Just words on a screen. Just a goddamned fantasy.

You're still logged on, so I'm going to assume you're reading this. We'd be alone—I wouldn't do what I plan on doing in front of a crowd. But I'll strip you, because I like you naked. And then I'll lead you over to a bench, and I'll ask you to spread yourself, faceup, and then I'll tie you down once you've given your consent.

Face up. Shit. Mal frowned. *Suppose I won't.*

I figured you'd play like that, Mal. If you want to fight me, go right ahead. I'm more than happy to restrain you, because no matter how unwilling you appear, I know how goddamned willing you are.

Try it.

You'd try to bolt, but I'd grab you. Hold you down until you stopped struggling. Stroke your cock through your pants until you're goddamned hard. I'd tell you you're doing a good job for me. That I've got you. You're not going anywhere, so maybe just try to enjoy it.

Fuck you.

Ah, no, that would be you this time.

Mal swallowed.

Right. See? No more fighting. You'd let me lead you to the bench, still holding your cock. I'd pinch your nipples before I started chaining you down—I need you very secure for this.

Mal pictured himself under Cillian's rein, spreading his legs for the man, his arms stretched overhead, uncomfortable but not terribly so.

But for now, he was pretending this had nothing to do with real life.

I'm sliding a small pillow under your ass. There, perfect. You're on display for me. Now I'm sliding a finger along your crack. The lube's warmed, and you're so ready for me.

Mal swore Cillian's finger was inside of him, rubbing, teasing. Yeah, he'd give himself over to this. Just once.

You haven't fought me—you just earned three fingers.

God. Fuck. He arched as he pulled at his cock, imagining how three would feel—leave him full, but not that full.

You're not touching yourself, are you, Mal? Because you're with me, and you're tied up.

Not touching.

Are you lying? I punish liars.

Good. He held his breath, waiting for Cillian's words to appear.

You just want to be over my lap. Not yet. Just open for me now, Mal. That's it . . . four fingers inside.

Mal stilled. *I can't.*

You can. You will. Four fingers are already impaling you. Not much you can do about it.

Mal squirmed, his ass rippling and tightening as he tried to stop the helplessness from flooding him.

One slight twist and I'm at the widest part of my hand.

No. Please.

Yes. Just breathe. Relax.

Mal gripped the side of the chair as though feeling the hand press into his ass. He hadn't been in this position for a very long time, and now, he wanted it. Needed it. Wished it was real, and yet it felt so goddamned real.

I'm in, baby. My whole hand's inside of you.

No.

I'm up to my wrist. Some of my forearm. God, you're so tight around me. Go ahead and look.

I can't.

You have to.

Mal was palming himself, his cock leaking. *Okay.*

That's it, baby. Look down.

Fuck. Mal pictured the scene in his mind . . . could real life ever be as fucking good? If it ever had, the memory would always pale in comparison to this moment.

I'm opening my hand now . . .

Mal came, an almost painful orgasm that put the earth back into its right orbit and left his head spinning. He gasped for air as he held on to the chair's arms, squinted to read Cillian's words . . .

I'm right here. I've got you.

Shit. Motherfucking son of a bitch goddamned asshole. He sucked in a few shaky breaths and typed, *Okay.*

Close your eyes. Relax.

He did, damn it. Pictured Cillian pulling out, then cleaning him, covering him. Just fucking being there for him. He sat there, not bothering to clean himself up because he was sure moving would break the spell, and he didn't want that yet.

It would happen soon enough, anyway.

CHAPTER NINE

Cillian had expected Mal to log off the second he'd typed, *Relax*, but Mal was still online. Just silent.

Before Mal's *Hey*, Cillian had been spiraling, spinning. And no matter how strange it seemed, Mal was apparently the most stable, immovable object in his life at the moment. So Cillian had grabbed on with both hands and used Mal to regain his focus.

It appeared, based on their previous conversations, that Mal had been using him for the same reasons.

In many ways, Mal was a world apart from Cillian.

In so many more ways, they were the same.

Cillian waited, allowing Mal a bit of time to pull himself together, then asked, *Are you all right?*

No. But I didn't expect to be.

Want to talk about it?

No.

He snorted. Should've seen that coming. *Fine.*

And then there was nothing for a long moment before Mal's next words appeared. *So that's how you do it.*

Do what?

Keep guys at arm's length. You act like their therapist.

And what do you do?

I just cut off contact.

But you haven't yet.

I'm too busy amusing myself watching you try to figure me out.

"You little shit," Cillian murmured, and he admitted to himself that was precisely one of the reasons he hadn't cut off communications himself. Because this was fun, and it had been a while since anything had been, at least for longer than an hour.

Because even though Mal was behind a screen—or probably *because* he was—Mal was the safest thing happening in Cillian's world right now.

And Cillian?

Yes?

It helped.

Cillian couldn't stop the small smirk he wore, knew it looked arrogant as hell—because it was. Because he was damned good at this, although he'd never actually put his personal life skills to use in his SB-20 work quite like this—to help someone besides himself.

If he was honest with himself, he'd have to admit he was also a bit relieved that Mal was okay after all that.

For a long moment, there was just silence and the blinking cursor. And then Mal's words appeared. *Spoke to my dad today. He needed to have a "come to Jesus" moment with me.*

How'd that go?

Jesus and I are still very far apart.

Cillian told himself to get the hell off the computer and not go any further into this. *Are you still heading out to LA?*

In a couple of weeks, yeah. Mal paused, and then, *I could've just not picked up the phone. I shouldn't have. But I did, because it was like I knew it was time to take my punishment. How fucked up is that?*

You could always be more fucked up, Mal.

Aren't we just a ray of sunshine.

Does it always go badly with your father?

Yes.

And it still gets to you.

Not every time. But this one . . .

Cillian shook his head. *Maybe making a clean break is necessary.*

We're tied together. It's complicated.

Everything is.

Mal's next words practically dripped sarcasm. *Oh look, now you *are* some kind of therapist.*

I've spent enough time with them to know.

My father's stubborn, Cillian.

Sounds like you've got a lot of him in you.

That's what happens when you grow up with someone.

Not born with it?

Not born to him.

Cillian started at the admission, wondering if Mal had meant to share that information. Then again, Cillian was good at interrogation whether or not he was trying to be . . . and even when he was goddamned lying to himself about this being nothing more than practice to that end.

And now he couldn't get Mal out of his mind. *Because he's not a threat to you*, he thought.

"Maybe, yes," he muttered to himself, but not entirely convincingly.

Connecting with a man over the computer was one thing—he'd done that before, most recently with Prophet, even though they hadn't quite managed to reach this level of personal intimacy. But Mal had nearly undone him in a very short time.

There was something about Mal, an odd transparency very different from the reindeer games operatives played.

Now he asked Mal, *When was the last time you were actually face-to-face with your father?*

Twelve years. Safer for us that way. Safer for me.

Cillian thought about Kasey, who, by all accounts was living with her father. So why wasn't it safe for Mal? *Why is that?*

My father and I never did see eye to eye.

Because you're gay?

For the record, I'm bi, but I don't think that mattered. He would've found something else. I'm just glad he took it all out on me and left my sister alone. She's the perfect one in his eyes and that's a good thing. Ah, fuck it, right? Can't let the past fuck up my future.

Didn't spare the rod, did he?

Mal paused and then . . . *What? Did you check with Prophet for my life story?*

Shit. Cillian's hand went to his shoulder, where he traced the old scars before typing, *You know what they say. Takes one to know one.*

His fingers froze for a long moment before he hit enter. Then he waited for what seemed like an eternity before Mal's answer popped up. *Gotta watch out for one another.*

Should he be more suspicious? Absolutely. Mal had somehow gotten to a place Cillian hadn't realized was still open and vulnerable.

But Mal had laid himself bare in the process. So the two of them were in the same boat. *I gather you're not always this forthcoming?*

Betting you're not either.

Cillian sighed. *I'm tired. You caught me on an off night.*

How did we go from cocks to this? Because I gotta tell you, cocks are more fun. Especially mine.

Cillian laughed.

CHAPTER TEN

The conversation left Mal wiped in a way he normally wasn't. He was always undercover, but this whole playing-a-role thing was harder. Which is why he typically avoided it.

He'd kept the lies as close to the truth as possible, which was actually why it wiped him. Because he'd let out too much of his truth. The only consolation was that it strengthened his cover—Cillian had latched onto it, since most operatives didn't talk about their childhoods, let alone shit like that.

But then the damned asshole had to go ahead and share . . .

Well, he could use that information, that vulnerability, no matter how much he hated to. Because he hadn't been lying to Cillian at all when he'd said that he believed that kids who'd been slammed around needed to stick together, from start to finish. And he spotted others of his kind so easily. Because he recognized that his inner child was so fucked that he never got a chance to come out and play

And Cillian could be lying to you completely. He could know exactly who you are. And that was the problem with trying to mindfuck someone who was as good as Cillian.

It was also part of the thrill. And his blood was definitely racing as he followed Cillian out of the hotel and for the several blocks to the same club where Mal had first seen him.

Cillian's confessional IM about visiting the club the other night hadn't surprised Mal because Mal had been following him, although he'd stopped short of going into the back room. Mal never liked these kinds of clubs, even when he was simply out for pleasure. Too many people, too much of everything. Since he'd lost his voice, he hated them even more. But there was a difference between hate and phobias, and Mal had no problem being in here for a job.

Keep telling yourself it's just a job, Mal.

Mal grabbed a scotch, let it sear down his throat and into his belly, enjoying the burn. He rarely drank these days, mainly because he needed to be alert all the damned time, but also because it made it so much easier to get a buzz on when he really needed it, like tonight.

It also made him forget his idea of going to the back room to let Cillian fuck him, because seriously, there was pushing boundaries, and then there was just flying over the edge without a net. And Mal had felt like he'd had wings *before* the scotch.

The alcohol forced him to be *more* conscious.

He put the glass down with a heavy thud, pushed past the two twinks who'd been trying to get into his pants—one of them to lift his wallet—and headed to the back room.

Cillian had already picked someone to fuck—a big bear of a man—and yeah, good move on waiting. Mal couldn't have handled Cillian touching him for real, especially not after the time he'd just spent online with the man. He could barely let the guy he picked put his hands on him. Instead, he pushed him, belly first, up against the wall, holding the guy's arms above his head with one hand.

He reached around with his other hand and tugged the guy's pants down, pushing them to the floor. Thankfully, neither of them were wearing underwear.

Mal squeezed the man's wrists, a signal for him to keep them there even when Mal let go to roll a condom on and use the sample lube packets he'd grabbed on his way into the back room.

Cillian was further along, already deep in his guy's ass, but when he dragged his eyes over to Mal, his fucking changed, his rhythm slowed, like he was waiting for Mal to catch up.

Heat flooded Mal's body—heat, followed by red-hot anger, at himself and at the spook for this entire fucking situation.

Cillian's earlier words had burned in his brain and echoed in his head now.

If you want to fight me, go right ahead. I'm more than happy to restrain you, because no matter how unwilling you appear, I know how goddamned willing you are.

He squirted lube on his fingers to open the waiting man up. The guy looked over his shoulder and down at Mal's dick, but when he went to talk, Mal grabbed his hair and turned his face back to the wall.

And then he glanced over at Cillian.

Mal, what the fuck are you doing?

But his internal warning didn't stop him, and when he entered the guy, his cock pulsing in the tight heat, he swore Cillian paused for a second, like he felt it too. Because in Mal's mind, he was fucking Cillian, driving deep into the man, the way he had once before.

Did Cillian remember him from the other night? Or was it just the thrill of the public sex, of knowing you were watching and being watched, that made Cillian's eyes glossy with lust and danger? No matter, because it drew Mal in like a goddamned homing device, a beacon, and they were fucking the men in front of them to the same rhythm. He grabbed the man's hips and bucked against him hard, and the man reached back to score his nails along Mal's neck, hitting that perfect pleasure-pain line. Mal hissed and leaned down to bite the man's neck as Cillian did the same to the man he was fucking.

Even though Mal was the one doing the fucking, he wasn't in control.

Then again, neither was Cillian. And that was Mal's only consolation.

When he came, in a roaring rush of blinding hot light, his entire body shuddered, his eyesight dimmed, but he didn't break from Cillian's gaze.

He told himself it was on purpose, and not that he couldn't— not that Cillian was holding him there with a laser-sharp focus that Mal knew could hold him for real, just like his typed commands had. And fuck yeah, his body yearned for that.

The first time Cillian had fucked inside a club had been for money, not pleasure.

Belgrade. He'd been sixteen, already providing sex for cash in alleyways and cars, but he'd finally moved up into the club leagues.

But it wasn't until he was seventeen and he'd started cruising the clubs for his own pleasure that he'd begun to realize his own power, how to use it, and why it was so important.

Until that point, Cillian had been a good drug mule, rentboy, and whatever else the man who'd clothed him, fed him, and sometimes paid him had asked of him. Good-looking, not too baby-faced, maybe because any innocence had been stripped so early in his life. That look had attracted a certain kind of client, and they'd happily paid to fuck him. Always in public, for Cillian's safety, because the man who took care of him wasn't stupid.

Neither was Cillian. Not for very long. Because that night, at seventeen, he learned about control—and needing it. Craving it.

Sauntered in, hard and unsatisfied, despite the fact that he was being screwed—and coming—several times a day. Part of that was teenage hormones. He could've fucked around the clock and still needed more.

He could easily pass for twenty. Boxing made him all taut, lanky muscles, strong and cocky. And that night he went into the back room, found a guy who was bigger than he was, and fucked the hell out of him.

He learned that there was just as much money to be made by actually being the one in control, turning the tables and surprising the hell out of the men. Ninety percent of the time, they enjoyed it. The other times taught Cillian to fight dirtier than he'd already known how to.

He also learned the subtleties of letting a man think he was in control when he wasn't.

Control had nothing to do with size or wealth. It was power. The head game, making the other person realize they really did want to give up control.

For him, that was the ultimate thrill. A hard-won victory for a scruffy street kid.

After that first fucking, he'd been jumped. Four men had followed him, and while he hadn't noticed them immediately, his instincts had kicked in halfway home. He'd ducked into an alleyway, and he'd been ready. Those fuckers hadn't been expecting to have the shit kicked out of them. And on a rainy, brutal afternoon, Cillian became a man far earlier than he should have.

He'd learned, but he'd paid a steep price for it. Which was why, today, Cillian preferred not to fuck in back rooms—too fraught with potential memories, especially if the sex wasn't good enough to obliterate them.

But tonight's sex had been. He couldn't be one hundred percent sure that the man who'd watched him had been his dark-haired man, but it didn't matter. In Cillian's mind, he was—and he was also Mal, and Cillian's fantasies had gone into overdrive.

Now, back at the hotel, showered, with room service at his side, and a night to himself, he thought about logging back into his IM and looking for Mal.

Cillian was looser with Mal. To say that he was no longer that street kid was as much of a lie as it would be to claim that the British spy persona was who he actually was. They were both a part of him, but whether he showed that to anyone was usually a conscious choice. With Mal, it hadn't been a choice at all.

Just because he was abused doesn't make him a match made in heaven.

Because Mal's past didn't include an orphanage in Belgrade, or being sold to various high bidders until he was old enough to break out on his own. But it did include scars that connected them through pain and a need for control, and the added bonus of an inability to trust beyond a certain point.

Mal was getting close to Cillian's limit on that.

Speaking of limits, Karl had canceled a meeting tonight. Cillian had texted Trent about it earlier, and now, he played the voice mail message Trent had left him while he was in the back room.

"You're screwing this up, Cillian," Trent's voice warned. "If you keep losing informants at this rate, you'll be starting from scratch and you'll have nothing."

"That's not true and you know it, Trent," he said out loud to no one and deleted Trent's message.

Trent sounded desperate. But true desperation wasn't something Cillian could successfully explain to anyone. People who hadn't lived through it never understood, but the weight of their judgment? That was ever present.

His handler was light years away from the slums.

The carnage Cillian had been responsible for haunted his waking moments, but never his dreams. Because he never dreamed. After a head injury he'd sustained thanks to a misstep during his dealing days, his dreams were gone.

Before he could stop himself, he typed to Mal, *Went out for a while.*

Like the other night? Because I got that message, loud and clear.

Cillian sighed, because he didn't know what the hell he'd told Mal that for. Had he been trying to tell Mal not to get too attached—or was he trying to remind himself?

Or had he really wanted Mal to know that he'd fucked a guy and pretended it was Mal? Now, all he typed was, *Yes, just like that.*

Did it help?

Now who's the therapist?

I learn from the best.

Sometimes fucking someone in person's good. Sometimes, it's not as good as through a computer screen.

He didn't get a response, and he wondered if Mal was out every night, getting screwed against the wall in various clubs, the way Cillian was out screwing, and even though he had no right to be jealous, he was. *When does your job start?*

Two days. I leave here tomorrow.

Cillian logged in to Prophet's apartment, scanned until he caught sight of the man, stretched on his belly on Prophet's bed. Back to the camera. As tempted as Cillian was to ask Mal to turn around and face the camera, he didn't. Instead, he turned the camera off, and said, *I'd like to visit you in LA.*

Like, IM visit or real life?

Real life. If you're up for it.

I don't know. I have to think about it.

I won't force you.

Ah, fuck that, Cillian. I know how this works. Eventually, because of whatever the hell it is you do, you'll shut me out. And fuck me, but this wasn't supposed to be anything. You couldn't just send me a dick picture like you were supposed to, right?

Yes, this is all my fault. He paused. *Have you ever done something you wished you could take back?*

All the time. I think that's pretty common for us regular folks too, Cillian.

"You have no idea," he muttered.

CHAPTER ELEVEN

"I'll tell you everything, man. Everything."

The man named Karl Johnston—the same one Mal had spied sitting next to Cillian at the bar that very first night they'd fucked—had tried to outmaneuver Mal for the past day. Now that Karl was caught, he'd go down the easiest of the three.

"Better yet, I can hook you up with my guy. He'd really like you—he likes guys who take the initiative."

His guy. John Morse. And yeah, John would fucking love Mal's *initiative*. He was going to goddamned eat that initiative one day in the not-so-distant future.

Mal held up the card and pointed the end of the gun to it, then to Karl's head.

"Come on, man . . . we can work something out. I can tell you shit."

But Karl was too late to the goddamned party, because Mal had learned that John was alive from Shelby, the first of Cillian's informants he'd taken down. He'd also learned that John had told Shelby, Peter, and Karl to kill Cillian, figuring, no doubt, that one of the three would get the job done. And even though Shelby and Karl knew each other, Mal would bet anything John had made them promise not to tell the others. John had that way of making whoever he'd focused his attention on feel special. Could charm the skin off a snake, as Mal's mother used to say.

Karl was still begging, half-crying, and it was getting boring as hell. Mal had no sympathy for a man who turned as easily as Karl had, and for a paltry sum of money. Now, he shut Karl up by going through his wallet, fishing out the key to the safety deposit box. Mal had stolen it hours earlier from Karl, gotten access to what he'd needed, and placed the key back in Karl's wallet. He'd done the same to Shelby and to Peter, just to make sure they were in fact working for John and all in on the plan to watch—and kill—Cillian.

"I know who your guy is." Mal sounded out the words slowly, using only his breath to make Karl understand, and he heard his own soft, garbled whisper. Maybe the injections were working.

Karl stared at him, silently. Mal bared his throat, pointed to the scar, and managed, "Your. Guy," near silently.

Karl's eyes widened. "Jesus. No."

Jesus, yes.

"I don't know who you are," Karl babbled. "I'm only supposed to kill Cillian—I don't have orders to hurt anyone else."

Mal sounded out, "Cillian . . . and John . . . working . . . together?"

He'd asked the other two men the same question, and he got a similar response now to what he'd gotten from them. "No way. John caught me, wanted to use me himself. He says I'm one of the best informants he's seen. John and Sadiq pay really well, man. I can try to get you in with them—they always need muscle."

Mal shook his head, pointed to the words, and then trained his gun on Karl's forehead. And only then did he turn on the video camera that was also pointed directly at Karl. The only thing it would capture of Mal was his hand, and the gun.

"He says he knows . . . the plan. He knows the truth. He knows you're alive, John. And he's coming for you."

Mal fired, a clean enough shot to the head that didn't have Karl suffering, even though the asshole deserved to, if for no other reason than for being greedy and supremely stupid.

Mal knew why he was killing these men. They had John's stink all over them—and once you were on a terrorist's payroll, you were fair fucking game. There was no turning back. Never had been, not for these men and not for him either. Not from day one of meeting John Morse and Prophet Drews on the field. John had been using his charm to lead Karl and the other informants on, just like he'd done to everyone who'd ever helped him.

And since Mal had gotten his proof that John was alive from Shelby, he'd also been using their deaths to send messages back to the asshole.

As to whether or not Cillian would figure out what was going on? That was a crapshoot. The fact that it'd been a seventy-two-hour whirlwind since Shelby's death made it difficult for even the most seasoned spook to figure shit out.

Really got you turned around, don't I, Cillian?

It would stay that way. He snapped the picture from Karl's phone, attached the video, and prepped the text to send in a couple of hours to Cillian. The spook had to think the messages were for him, at least in part. And Mal had John's number on his own phone now, because he wasn't hiding from the fucker. He'd send this video to him immediately.

He peeled the latex gloves from his fingers, bagged them so he could burn them, and walked back to the hotel where Cillian was two floors below and three rooms to the left. Once in his own room, he sank onto the bed.

For a long moment, he lay there, staring at a minuscule crack that had begun to reach from one end of the ceiling to the other. Cracks were always there; no matter how well repaired, there would always be weakness.

Discovering he'd been right about John's betrayal of Prophet, of the rest of the team, how John had been complicit in a terrorist plot to kidnap a high-level nuclear physicist, should've left him spinning. It hadn't, because Mal had always goddamned known it, on many levels. But now the proof was indisputable.

He headed to the shower to wash the smell of blood, fear, and latex from his skin. When he got out, his skin was flushed from the heat, and he dried himself roughly, touching the reaper tattoo on his back the way he always did—part luck, all superstition, his own personal sign of the cross.

And then he went to his open laptop, fed into Prophet's apartment . . . and saw Cillian was logged in to IM. He dressed in a pair of jeans and a wifebeater, shoved his feet into his favorite black shit-kicking boots and grabbed a thermal shirt, but didn't put it on.

Cillian's conversations with Prophet were different from those he had with Mal. For all the chemistry between his friend and the spook, and you'd have to be dead not to see it, they hadn't acted on it. And there were so many times they could've. But with Mal, Cillian had.

Because the guy behind the spook gets me. That stunned Mal, because no one ever really had. They got parts of him, most of him, but Cillian got him so completely that it actually hurt to be so exposed.

Speaking of exposed, he glanced at the opened laptop.

This could go so fucking wrong, Mal, he told himself.

But what else was new. He had to trust in Cillian's patterns, his vulnerabilities . . . the fact that the spook was off-center. It was up to Mal to push him the rest of the way down.

He sat heavily and typed, *You there?*

After several long moments, Cillian responded with, *I never left.*

Bad night?

How was yours?

Point taken. So why don't you get on your goddamned knees, Cillian, and let me help?

I'm already there, Mal.

Where you belong.

There was a significant pause, and then Cillian's response came through. *You think, because I'm on my knees, that I'm not in control. Come on, Mal. Maybe no one else has given you the credit you deserve, but I will. You're a manipulative shit. You make it so people believe you're in control, so you can let yourself go and they won't notice. I notice everything. I know you're not in control here, nor do you want to be. Not the majority of the time. I also know there's nothing goddamned wrong with that—or you.*

Mal sat back, heaving like he'd been punched. He'd never stayed with anyone long enough for them to find this out. He hadn't been with Cillian long enough either . . .

Don't you dare close that computer and try to run from me, Cillian typed. *I will find you.*

Mal shuddered. Typed *here* with one finger.

Good. Breathe. Take your time, sit there and stare at my words. Do not leave.

Order?

Does it really need clarification?

Yes.

You will drive me to drink. Yes, Mal, it's an order. So is the one to go back and read my words while you jack yourself off, realizing I've caught you.

Don't do this to me.

What? Call you out? Know you? Give you pleasure? Give me a reasonable answer as to why I shouldn't, and I won't.

Mal's fingers hovered above the keys, the danger churning through his mind and body, making him reckless and sure of himself at the same time. Typed *I can't*, hit enter, and then left the room and the hotel without looking back, all the while hoping Cillian was worked up enough to follow his familiar pattern of heading to the club.

Because what Mal was doing now was far less about his job, and everything to do with figuring out just how far he'd let Cillian into his system. And whether or not he had a shot of getting him out anytime soon.

CHAPTER TWELVE

Cillian walked into the bar ten minutes later, most obviously on the prowl.

Mal hated being the prey. Nervousness choked him, and he downed two whiskeys and palmed a third as he cut through the crowds to get ahead of the man dressed in all black and into the back room.

Unlike last night, it was packed—wall-to-wall bodies, undulating and groaning in the semidarkness, and Mal almost turned around.

Actually, he tried to, but he found himself face-to-face with Cillian. A brief flash of panic had him wondering if Cillian had been playing him the entire time . . .

Until the spook said, "I saw you here last night," and ran a thumb across Mal's lower lip. Mal shuddered, relief and arousal catching him by the throat all at once. "I was hoping I'd find you here again."

Mal just stared, because this was too close for comfort. And even though he'd planned it, down to this goddamned minute, the realness of it threatened every reserve he'd ever had. Because the endgame had suddenly changed—and it continued to flip on him every time he tried to come to grips with it. Because Cillian wasn't working for John—and if he wasn't working for the guy, the only possible reason he'd have to follow him, and trace Prophet's moves, was to kill John. Which made Cillian a whole lot less of a fucking asshole in Mal's book.

When Cillian moved his hand, Mal drew in a stuttered breath that he didn't think Cillian would hear. But the man caught everything, leaned close to Mal's ear, and asked, "Are you scared?"

Mal closed his eyes, breathed in Cillian's scent, and nodded against the man's cheek, his heart pounding a thousand miles an hour, despite knowing that nothing heavy would go down in this room. This wasn't that kind of place . . . but letting Cillian in, that was heavy enough.

"Don't be scared. Let me take care of everything." With that, his hand rested on Mal's nape, and Mal allowed himself to be led deeper into the room. When they got to the very back wall, Cillian pushed aside a few men and edged Mal into place. The men were so deep into their fucking that they didn't seem to notice being moved a couple of feet.

"Is that what you want?" Cillian asked as Mal stared at the men going at it, one of them with his legs locked around the other man's waist.

Mal glanced at him and then attempted to turn and face the wall.

But Cillian caught him. It was even darker in this corner, too dark to see more than the shadows of faces. But Mal caught a glint of power in Cillian's eyes before Cillian crushed his mouth to Mal's with a kiss that tasted like the fine scotch Cillian drank and a hint of lemon and wealth. Because wealth had a damned taste.

This had been a severe miscalculation on Mal's part. Of course, he could push Cillian off and walk out, sever the ties, and save himself. But he didn't want to.

Instead, he let Cillian manhandle the fuck out of him, which started as Cillian's hands circled his wrists, holding them down to his sides, pressing his back to the wall and their cocks together through the fabric of their pants.

When Cillian tried to break the kiss, Mal caught his lower lip between his teeth and tugged, held on for a few seconds longer than necessary before allowing Cillian to pull away completely. Cillian smirked, murmured, "Fucking brat," and then let go of Mal's wrists long enough to turn him roughly against the wall.

Mal brought his hands up automatically to catch himself.

"That's good. Put them higher," Cillian told him, and Mal did as he was told. He'd already begun to sweat, a trickle down his back. Cillian's arm wound around his waist, tugged his pants open with very little effort, and murmured appreciatively. Mal heard the rip of a condom, felt the chill of lube on Cillian's fingertips as they trailed along Mal's crack and began to spread him, one finger first and then two.

Mal shuddered.

"Don't you come yet, greedy thing," Cillian admonished, and Mal hissed silently as a third finger took him. He went up on his toes to escape the pressure, but Cillian guided him firmly down with a hand on his shoulder. A fingertip rubbed Mal's gland, jolting him. Cillian wrapped a hand around the base of his cock to stop any potential orgasm, and Mal breathed in relief. He didn't want to come that soon.

"Good, baby," Cillian crooned as he replaced his fingers with the fat crown of his cock, pushing up against the natural resistance of Mal's body. Instead of trying to escape it, Mal pushed back, letting his ass open for the man's entrance. As Cillian filled him, Mal hung on to the wall for dear fucking life.

Cillian took him at a brutal pace that owned Mal, a primal goddamned rhythm. Mal bit Cillian's arm, because he could, because the man was goddamned big. Because Mal was picturing what else Cillian could put inside him.

"That's it—you just give yourself to me," Cillian soothed, the words the opposite of the fucking. Mal closed his eyes and silently whimpered. Surrendered in a way that Cillian had to feel, because he swore through clenched teeth.

And then Cillian's arm clamped around Mal's shoulders, the other on his hips, stopping Mal from doing much more than taking every single stroke. But it managed to be a cradling hold too, one that Mal hadn't been aware he'd needed until that moment, especially when the spook murmured, "That's it. Goddammit, Mal."

Mal jerked his head back with surprise, but Cillian murmured, "Not a word. For tonight, that's your name."

Mal nodded . . . something nagged at him between the flush of heat and pride, but then he immediately lost the thought in his sudden, fierce orgasm. Cillian's wasn't far behind, and he finished with harsh breaths in Mal's ear as his body jerked through its climax.

CHAPTER THIRTEEN

Cillian held Mal for several moments after they came, and Mal had to force himself not to nuzzle the guy's cheek. Finally, Cillian released him and walked away. Without looking in the spook's direction, Mal knew the man hadn't looked back at him. It didn't matter—Cillian's head was with Mal.

He pushed away from the wall and went out the back exit of the club, the alarm ringing for a brief moment behind him. He was there when Cillian walked past the alleyway's entrance, going in the opposite direction from their hotel.

He also saw the man on Cillian's six.

Was there another informant? As Mal trailed him, he checked the phone he'd linked to Cillian's and saw no messages, not even the one about Karl. That one would come through in less than half an hour.

Now, Mal rounded the corner, preparing to stop the man from getting too close to Cillian, when he realized that Cillian had disappeared inside a doorway. Mal moved to follow him, then halted dead in his tracks, hidden in the shadows of the abandoned building's crumbling interior.

The man following Cillian had done the same, was about to circle back toward the exit where Mal was hiding, when an arm shot out from the dark and grabbed him. Mal saw the side view— Cillian, gripping the man by the hair, dragging his head back to expose his neck. He saw the glint of the blade off the streetlight that came through the broken windows.

"You weren't set to arrive until next week, Vince," Cillian said casually. "Then again, you've been telling me a lot of untruths. I suspect that working for a terrorist like John Morse has led you down the wrong path."

Cillian *had* figured it out—all of it. Or else he'd suspected and was now using Vince's terror as confirmation. Because Mal knew the smell of fear intimately.

Vince remained perfectly still in Cillian's grip, the smart thing to do when a blade was pressed to your throat. Mal began to sweat, swore he already smelled the metallic tang of the blood, even though he didn't think Cillian had made a cut yet.

And Cillian ... he stared down at the man and then the knife, as if contemplating something. His hand nearly shook, like he was trying to slash across the man's throat. But ultimately, he pulled the knife back and stuck it cleanly into the man's carotid, and as the man struggled against him, said clearly, *"Is mise mo namhaid is measa."*

Mal's head swam at the familiar words—the accent that he'd caught the briefest hint of back at the club ... the voice from all those years ago ...

I am my own worst enemy.

He leaned his forehead against the old plaster. When he finally looked up, Cillian was gone, and Vince was lying in a puddle of blood on the floor.

CHAPTER FOURTEEN

Mal wasn't sure how he made it back to the hotel, but when he latched the door behind him, he grabbed the wall, the way he'd done in the club, palms spread, and tried to breathe. His vision was a haze, his throat burned, and he could still smell Cillian all over him.

Could still hear Cillian's voice echoing around him.

Is mise mo namhaid is measa. I am my own worst enemy.

His throat burned, like it had just been slashed. Again. Every inch of him wanted to slam his fists through the wall, to break every bone in his hands, his feet. It was like no time at all had passed since Cillian—God, Cillian, not John—had slit his throat and left him to die without a backward glance.

Cillian.

That night, three years ago, *Cillian* had come up from behind Mal, who'd been so intent on waiting for John that he'd failed to notice that someone else was already waiting.

Waiting for John? Or waiting for Mal?

That was the part Mal still didn't know. But he'd looked an awful lot like John at the time, because he'd dyed his hair blond and worn colored contacts. He figured if he looked enough like John Morse, maybe someone would mistake him for John and give him a solid lead.

And he'd gotten part of what he'd wished for. Because, at the time, Mal hadn't had any proof that John was alive, other than his inherent suspicion and a radar he'd been born with. He had to assume John had known Mal was attempting to smoke him out. Had to assume John had been following him, setting him up, letting Cillian know exactly where to find him. A giant game of cat and mouse and Mal had fucked up. *Had*. Past fucking tense. And now, both Cillian and John would get what was coming to them.

But it wasn't like Mal would ever have closure.

His hands fisted against the wall. He could still feel Cillian's hands on him, capable and strong. Hands of a killer.

Mal looked up at his own hands like he didn't recognize them for a second, and then he pushed off the wall and let them travel the way Cillian's had, under his shirt, up his chest. But Cillian's hands had stopped after pinching his nipples and traveled back down. Mal stripped his shirt so his hands could keep going, all the way to his throat, touching the thick scar.

Cillian's hands in his hair, stretching his neck back. Cillian's—not John's.

"Is mise mo namhaid is measa."

The first slice.

Mal's throat hadn't been cut cleanly. No, his attacker had made several, torturous cuts, deep enough to harm, but not kill immediately. Cillian had expected him to bleed out but had wanted it to happen slowly.

And he would've died, if King hadn't found him. So Cillian's sadism had saved Mal's life.

When Mal had hit the ground, dying, he'd rolled to escape the blade. He'd seen everything through a thick haze but he'd sworn he'd heard footsteps. They'd sounded like they were getting fainter, were leaving, but when he'd looked up, he'd sworn John was staring down at him. Smiling.

But because Mal had never been able to distinguish that as reality or not, he'd never told Proph, because why dig the knife in deeper?

And now, he'd dug the knife deeper for himself just fine. And he liked it.

I am my own worst enemy.

Mal forced himself over to the computer, opened up his IM program, and waited.

CHAPTER FIFTEEN

illian's hands were still shaking. He couldn't afford to leave people alive these days, but he usually also couldn't bring himself to use a knife. Only under extreme circumstances and when he was cornered, and today definitely qualified as both.

He'd wiped the knife of prints and blood and tossed it into the river. The police had enough to do in this country besides solve murders of known informants who worked for international terrorists, even terrorists who weren't supposed to exist. Vince Kelly had been with Cillian for over three years, since the start of his mission, and he'd had some damned good hits on John over the years, the last one being four months earlier.

Cillian could only assume that's when John had caught up to Vince, and Vince had turned easily. And why not? Money was money.

He called Trent now. "Vince Kelly tried to kill me. He must have been turned by John. I'm going to assume the other two were as well."

"You should've figured this out sooner, Cillian, instead of finding time to fuck."

"You had me followed?"

"Not at all. I know your reputation, and you just confirmed it." Trent sounded oddly pleased with himself.

"Fuck you, Trent," he hissed, not caring that the brogue came through. He cared about that less and less, he realized, because once John was gone, the carefully constructed spy persona would go away too, leaving behind the wild Irish boy he'd always been inside. And if the SB-20 team didn't want him anymore, they could go fuck themselves.

"Ah, come on, Cillian—you used to be able to take a joke."

"None of this is anything to joke about."

"No, it's not," Trent told him, just as a video of Karl came through Cillian's phone.

"The other three," Cillian breathed. "All four of them."

"Three what? Four what?" Trent demanded as Cillian managed to dock the phone so they could watch the video together. Cillian couldn't look away from the screen. He watched the barrel of the gun hovering near Karl's head. But nothing happened until Karl looked at the camera and repeated the words Shelby and Peter had been forced to say before him.

He knows the plan. He knows the truth.

"What the hell, Cillian?" Trent muttered, but Cillian hushed him. Because he finally knew. The plan was that Morse had told Shelby, Peter, and Karl—and no doubt Vince—to kill Cillian.

The truth was that Morse was still alive. And the only person Cillian had lied to about that was Prophet. Who had no doubt told his teammates.

Whoever had killed Cillian's informants had saved Cillian's life.

When he'd lived on the streets, the rule was live or die—there was no in between and it was as simple as that. The spy game was that simple too, and that's why he was so good at it.

But there was always someone better. Someone who wanted it more. Someone who'd get it, take it from you, and leave you lying dead in the street.

At one time, he'd *been* that someone. But then he'd killed an innocent man Morse had placed in his path. He'd slit the man's throat without remorse, and then, when he'd realized it wasn't Morse, he'd left him there to bleed out, and all because he hadn't wanted Morse's trail to get cold.

He'd missed Morse by three minutes. Three minutes and the helo had already been too far to shoot down.

He'd almost retired because of that but here he was, three years later, still tracking down that fucking traitor.

He glanced down from the video to the minimized IM screen. He clicked it open, and Trent's cursing faded into the background as he saw a picture of a dark-haired, roughly handsome man staring back at him, a self-satisfied smirk on his face that didn't reach his haunted eyes.

The man in the picture was the man from the club. The man he'd fucked and been fucked by in the club.

Cillian blinked as the picture changed, showcasing the same brutally handsome man staring at him, a knowing, cocky gaze, but this time with his chin lifted enough to expose the scar on his neck.

And he was holding the knife Cillian had dropped next to the body of the innocent man in his race to catch Morse.

He could no longer be mistaken for Morse, of course. The blond hair was gone. The contacts too.

But the scar . . .

Cillian's hands shook as a piece of paper with the phrase *Is mise mo namhaid is measa* on it replaced the face . . . the scar.

He'd spoken those words tonight when he'd killed Vince. He'd also spoken them many times in his life when he'd killed people—but not since the night he'd killed an innocent man.

The night he *thought* he'd killed an innocent man.

Because Cillian was quite sure that the innocent man—the one who haunted his waking hours—had killed all his informants, saving his life. That innocent man—who was maybe not so innocent—had taken the picture of Cillian next to Shelby's body. He'd taken videos of himself killing Peter and Karl. And he must have been *right there* when Cillian had killed Vince, because the words he'd said when Vince had fallen to the ground were staring at him right now.

Right next to Mal's dick pic avatar.

Explore the Universe of *Extreme Escapes, Ltd.*

riptidepublishing.com/titles/universe/extreme-escapes-ltd

Catch a Ghost
ISBN: 978-1-62649-039-0

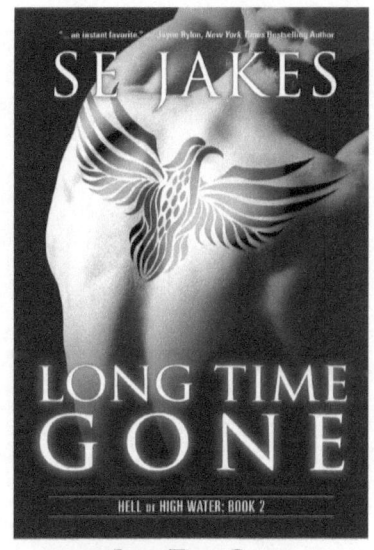

Long Time Gone
ISBN: 978-1-62649-061-1

Daylight Again
ISBN: 978-1-62649-141-0

Free Falling
ISBN: 978-1-62649-137-3

Dear Reader,

Thank you for reading SE Jakes' *Dirty Deeds*!

We know your time is precious and you have many, many entertainment options, so it means a lot that you've chosen to spend your time reading. We really hope you enjoyed it.

We'd be honored if you'd consider posting a review—good or bad—on sites like **Amazon, Barnes & Noble, Kobo, Goodreads, Twitter, Facebook, Tumblr,** and your blog or website. We'd also be honored if you told your friends and family about this book. Word of mouth is a book's lifeblood!

For more information on upcoming releases, author interviews, blog tours, contests, giveaways, and more, please sign up for our weekly, spam-free newsletter and visit us around the web:

Newsletter: tinyurl.com/RiptideSignup
Twitter: twitter.com/RiptideBooks
Facebook: facebook.com/RiptidePublishing
Goodreads: tinyurl.com/RiptideOnGoodreads
Tumblr: riptidepublishing.tumblr.com

Thank you so much for Reading the Rainbow!

RiptidePublishing.com

ACKNOWLEDGMENTS

For the Riptide crew—here goes: For Sarah Frantz, because I promise her an uncomplicated book every time, and she humors me. Every. Time. For Rachel Haimowitz, because being both creative and a businesswoman is a thing to see. For Keturah Jenkins, who handles all the aspects of marketing and generally puts my ducks in a row. For L.C. Chase, because the covers and layouts are to die for. For everyone behind the scenes, just thank you.

For my Ask SEJ girls, especially my regulars, because the discussions we have keep me going. For all my readers, because your support is incredible.

And, as always, for my family, because without them, none of this would ever happen.

ALSO BY SE JAKES

Havoc Motorcycle Club
Running Wild

Hell or High Water (EE, Ltd.) Series
Catch a Ghost
Long Time Gone
Daylight Again
Not Fade Away
If I Ever (Coming soon)

Men of Honor Series
Bound by Honor
Bound by Law
Ties That Bind
Bound by Danger
Bound for Keeps (EE, Ltd.)
Bound to Break

Standalone
Free Falling (EE, Ltd.)

ABOUT THE AUTHOR

SE Jakes writes m/m romance. She believes in happy endings and fighting for what you want in both fiction and real life. She lives in New York with her family and most days, she can be found happily writing (in bed). No really . . .

SE Jakes is the pen name of *New York Times* best-selling author Stephanie Tyler (and half of Sydney Croft).

You can contact her the following ways:

Email: authorsejakes@gmail.com

Website: sejakes.com

Tumblr: sejakes.tumblr.com

Facebook: Facebook.com/SEJakes

Twitter: Twitter.com/authorsejakes

Instagram: instagram.com/authorsejakes

Goodreads Group: Ask SE Jakes

Truth be told, the best way to contact her is by email or in blog comments. She spends most of her time writing but she loves to hear from readers!

Enjoy more stories like
Dirty Deeds
at RiptidePublishing.com!